一個購物情境，多種說法，快速掌握臨時需要的那句購物英文

出國血拼，臨時需要的那句英文

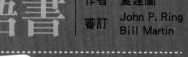

最實用的購物英語書

作者　夏建蘭

審訂　John P. Ring
　　　Bill Martin

U0123621

2000 句實用逛街購物句型，讓你像老外一樣說英文

怕說英文？

在非英語系國家裡，「開口說」常常是學習者的一大障礙。不論是初學或學了十多年英語，很多人都會因為自覺發音不標準、擔心文法用錯、怕鬧笑話而「不敢說」。

本書幫助你說出道地英語

由兩位資深專業外籍英文教師審訂的這本會話書，完全符合國外情境，句子都是老外在逛街購物時會說的，所以跟著本書學習，不用擔心學到中式英文。作者針對台灣的英語學習者「沒有自信、不敢開口」的問題，精心設計情境會話，依照不同情境發展出各種單元，讓讀者可隨時參閱，每個單元裡都有以下豐富的內容：

1. 這句可以這麼說：針對特定逛街購物情境最常說的一句話，提供多句同義但說法不同的句子，方便替代使用。
2. 學學老外這麼說：生動的實境對話，讓你掌握句子使用的場合，了解對話發展的脈絡。
3. 單字、片語：實用單字、老外常用的片語，讓你的英語說得更道地。
4. 情境插圖：搭配會話繪製的生動插圖，加深聯結記憶，減輕學習負擔。
5. MP3 會話錄音：會說正確句子，也要學會正確發音、語調。聆聽專業外籍錄音員錄製的會話，讓你會聽又會說。

要怎樣跟老外說得一樣？

這本書集結了各種逛街購物實用會話，全是老外平日在用的句子，讀者不必擔心在哪個場合要說什麼、怎麼說才道地。這本書裡沒有艱深的文法、沒有困難的用字，不必煩惱看不懂，MP3 裡還有正確的腔調與發音可供隨時聆聽，只要你敢開口，英文就能說得像老外一樣，看懂國外最新最潮的情報雜誌，了解歐美時尚背後的真意，再也不是難事！

如何使用本書

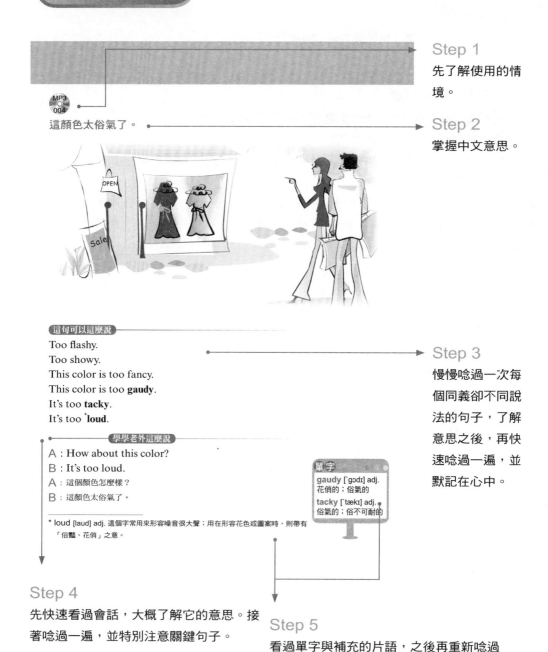

MP3
004

這顏色太俗氣了。

這句可以這麼說

Too flashy.
Too showy.
This color is too fancy.
This color is too **gaudy**.
It's too **tacky**.
It's too *loud.

學學老外這麼說

A : How about this color?
B : It's too loud.
A : 這個顏色怎麼樣？
B : 這顏色太俗氣了。

----
* loud [laud] adj. 這個字常用來形容噪音很大聲；用在形容花色或圖案時，則帶有
　「俗豔、花俏」之意。

單字
gaudy [ˋgɔdɪ] adj.
花俏的；俗氣的
tacky [ˋtækɪ] adj.
俗氣的；俗不可耐的

Step 1
先了解使用的情境。

Step 2
掌握中文意思。

Step 3
慢慢唸過一次每個同義卻不同說法的句子，了解意思之後，再快速唸過一遍，並默記在心中。

Step 4
先快速看過會話，大概了解它的意思。接著唸過一遍，並特別注意關鍵句子。

Step 5
看過單字與補充的片語，之後再重新唸過一次會話，看看自己是否更能掌握句子的用法。

3

Step 6

搭配 MP3 使用，培養聽力與口說能力。

 MP3 使用建議

1. 先看過每篇主題內容，理解文意後，自己先大聲朗讀一遍。
2. 對照書裡的內容聆聽該軌 MP3。
3. 聆聽 MP3 時，試著不看書是否能完全聽懂。若不能，則重複第 2 步驟，直到完全聽懂為止。
4. 在反覆聆聽 MP3 的同時，也留意錄音員的發音、語調，並跟著模仿練習。
5. 隨時隨地播放 MP3 內容，即使不是用心在聆聽，單字的發音、句子的語調都會在無形中深植於腦海中。

CONTENTS

風格

「浮華易逝，風格永存。（Fashions fade, but style is eternal.）」這似乎是時尚女子的偶像奧黛麗‧赫本一生的寫照，也將是時尚女子的永遠追求。風格不僅是那件「黑色晚禮服（black evening dress）」，那個「LV 包（a Louis Vuitton handbag）」，那副拉風的「防風眼鏡」（goggles）和那對「蒂芬尼耳環（Tiffany's post earring）」上耀眼的光芒，還有那件個性十足的「手工 T 恤（self-made T-shirt）」，和那笑臉上揚起的嘴角。時尚女子的口號是：「血拼（shopping）。」這不是終極目標，因為時尚並無極致，重要的是造就自我風格，述說美麗心情。

MP3
002

這件襯衫有藍色的嗎？

這句可以這麼說

Does this *blouse *come in blue?

Do you have a blue one?

Do you have this blouse in blue?

May I see a blue one in this style?

學學老外這麼說

A : Do you have this blouse in blue?

B : If you don't see one in the rack, I'll have to check the *stock room.

A : 這件女襯衫有藍色的嗎？

B : 如果貨架上沒有的話，我去查庫房。

---

* blouse [blaus] n. 特指女性襯衫。

* come in 後面接顏色、花紋、包裝方式、版本等，用來表示某項商品所提到的
  這些規格。

* stock room 庫房。

單字

stock [stɑk] n.
（商店的）存貨

MP3
003

我覺得那顏色不適合你。

這句可以這麼說

I don't think that's your color.
I don't think that color suits you.
I don't think you look good in that color.

學學老外這麼說

A：Should I buy this blue one?
B：I don't think that's your color.
A：我該買這件藍色的嗎？
B：我覺得那顏色不適合你。

MP3
004

這顏色太俗氣了。

Too flashy.
Too showy.
This color is too fancy.
This color is too **gaudy**.
It's too **tacky**.
It's too *loud.

A : How about this color?
B : It's too loud.

A : 這個顏色怎麼樣？
B : 這顏色太俗氣了。

單字

gaudy [ˋgɔdɪ] adj.
花俏的；俗氣的
tacky [ˋtækɪ] adj.
俗氣的；俗不可耐的

---

* loud [laud] adj. 這個字常用來形容噪音很大聲；用在形容花色或圖案時，則帶有
「俗豔、花俏」之意。

我最愛的衣服顏色

garnet 石榴紅色

emerald green 翠綠色

lilac 淺紫色

bisque 可可色

ivory 象牙色

smoky gray 煙灰色

navy blue 海軍藍；天藍色

apricot 杏黃色

coffee 咖啡色

chestnut brown 栗褐色

beige 米色

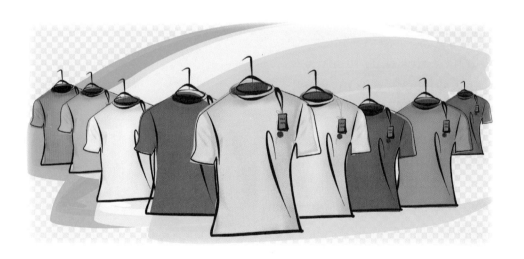

這件裙子有我的尺寸嗎？

這句可以這麼說

Do you have this skirt in my size?

Does this skirt come in my size?

學學老外這麼說

A : Can I help you?

B : Yes. Does this skirt come in my size?

A : Yes. Would you like to try it on?

B : Yes. Where is the *dressing room*?

A : 需要幫助嗎？

B : 是的。這件裙子有我的尺寸嗎？

A : 有。要試穿嗎？

B : 好。試衣間在哪裡？

---

* dressing room、fitting room 都指「試衣間」。但前者為英式用法，後者為美式用法。

MP3
006

你穿什麼尺寸？

這句可以這麼說

What size?

What's your size?

What size do you want / need?

What size do you wear?

Do you know what size you are?

學學老外這麼說

A：What size?

B：I am not sure. Can you take my *__measurements__?

A：Sure. You're a six.

A：你穿什麼尺寸？

B：我不太確定。你能幫我量一下嗎？

A：好的。你穿六號。

---

* measurement [ˋmɛʒɚmənt] n. 這個字原本是「測量」。若為複數形，則指「尺寸」或「（女性的）三圍」。

沒有你的尺寸。

這句可以這麼說

We don't have your size.

We don't have that in your size.

We're *sold out of your size.

Your size isn't available.

學學老外這麼說

A : Do you have this **top** in a size 6?

B : Let me check. Sorry. We don't have a size 6 in stock.

A : 這件上衣有六號的嗎？

B : 我查一查。抱歉，六號沒庫存了。

單字
top [tɑp] n. 上衣

---

* sold out 售完。

MP3 008

這件襯衫做工很好。

The **handiwork** on this blouse is **exquisite**.

The handiwork of this blouse is delicate.

This blouse has a nice cut.

This blouse is well-tailored.

學學老外這麼說

A : Your dress is **gorgeous**! The handiwork is so exquisite. Is it a *designer dress?

B : Thank you. It was a gift from my boyfriend. It's by the Ports.

A : 你的洋裝真漂亮！手工很精緻，是不是名牌的？

B : 謝謝。它是我男朋友送給我的，是寶姿的。

---

* designer dress 名牌服裝；設計師服裝。

單字

handiwork
[ˋhændɪˌwɝk] n.
手工

exquisite
[ˋɛkskwɪzɪt] adj.
精緻的

gorgeous
[ˋɡɔrdʒəs] adj.
（口）非常漂亮的

這件羊毛衫脫線了。

這句可以這麼說

This **cardigan** is coming apart at the **seams.**

This cardigan is bursting at the seams.

This cardigan is coming undone here.

The seams of this cardigan are coming *unstitched.

學學老外這麼說

A : I bought this cardigan this morning, but it's already coming apart at the seams.

B : I am terribly sorry. I'll get you another one.

A : I'd like to return it and get a **refund**.

A : 我上午剛買的這件羊毛衫脫線了。

B : 對不起，我給您換一件。

A : 我想退貨還款。

單字

cardigan
[ˈkɑrdɪɡən] n.
羊毛衫

seam [sim] n.
衣服縫邊

stitch [stɪtʃ] v.
將某物縫上

refund [ˈrɪˌfʌnd]
n. 退款

---

* stitch [stɪtʃ] v. 聯結，固定。unstitched 脫落，不固定。

這件羊毛衣洗完後縮水得厲害。

這句可以這麼說

This wool sweater **shrank** a lot after being washed.

This wool sweater was several sizes smaller after being washed.

I washed my wool sweater, and it shrank more than a size!

學學老外這麼說

A : This wool sweater I bought shrank 3 sizes.

B : Did you hand wash it in cold water?

A : No. I used a washing machine.

A：我買的這件羊毛衣縮了三號。

B：你是用冷水和手洗的嗎？

A：不是，我用洗衣機。

單字

shrink [ʃrɪŋk] v.
縮水

各式標籤和洗標

material 衣料材質

cotton 棉

silk 絲

wool 羊毛

cashmere 喀什米爾羊毛

fur & leather 毛皮

linen 麻

polyester 聚酯纖維

nylon 尼龍

acrylic 亞克力

lycra 彈性萊卡

Washing Symbols and Instructions 洗衣說明

machine wash 洗衣機水洗

hand wash 手洗

bleach when needed 必要時可漂白

tumble dry 可烘乾

do not wring 不可擰乾

iron 可熨燙

dry clean 可乾洗

spin dry, reshape, and dry flat 脫水後整平；平放晾乾

這件洋裝適合我嗎?

這句可以這麼說

Does this dress look good on me?

How do I look in this dress?

Do I look OK in this dress?

Does this dress look right on me?

學學老外這麼說

A : Do I look OK in this dress?

B : Not just OK. You look totally **glamorous**!

A : 這件洋裝適合我嗎?

B : 何止適合!簡直是光彩照人啊!

單字

glamorous
[ˋglæmərəs] adj.
漂亮的;形容女性有
魅力的

19

MP3
012

這種款式現在很流行。

這句可以這麼說

This style is ***in** now.

That is in this season.

This style is **all the rage** at the moment.

This is in style this year.

This style is quite popular at the moment.

學學老外這麼說

A : This style is all the rage at the moment. And it
seems like it was **tailored** to your shape.

B : I'll take it.

A : 這種款式現在很流行，簡直就像為你量身訂做的。

B : 那我買了。

---

* in（口）流行的；時尚的。

* range [rendʒ] n. 區域。all the rage 風行一時。

單字

tailor [`telə] v.
訂做，特別製作

這種款式已經過時了。

這句可以這麼說

That's ***out** of style now.

That has **gone out** of style.

That style is really out-dated.

That style is behind the times.

That is not this year's style.

This style has gone out of fashion.

學學老外這麼說

A : Her dress looks funny.

B : It looks fine to me.

A : Are you kidding? That style went out last year.

A : 她的洋裝看起來真好笑。

B : 我覺得挺好的。

A : 你開玩笑吧？那種款式去年就過時了。

---

* out（口）過時的；老土的。

* go out（口）過時。

飛鼠袖又開始流行了。

這句可以這麼說

*__Batwing sleeves__ are coming back into vogue.

Batwing sleeves are back in fashion.

Batwing sleeves are starting to catch on.

Batwing sleeves have caught on recently.

Batwing sleeves are experiencing a revival.

學學老外這麼說

A : Batwing sleeves have caught on recently.

B : Styles come and go so quickly. You know what never goes out? As the king of fashion, Yves Saint Laurent, said, "What a woman needs is a black turtleneck sweater, a straight skirt, and a man to love her."

A : 飛鼠袖最近又開始流行起來了。

B : 很快又會過時的。你知道什麼是永遠不過時的嗎？就像時尚界泰斗聖・羅蘭所說：「一個女人需要的，就是一件黑色高領毛衣、直筒裙，和一個愛她的男人。」

---

* batwing [ˋbætwɪŋ] adj. 像蝙蝠翅膀的。batwing sleeves 飛鼠袖（的服裝）。

MP3
015

我想買新衣服。

I wish to buy a new **wardrobe**.

I want to update my wardrobe.

I want to add some new items to my wardrobe.

學學老外這麼說

A : I really want to update my wardrobe.

B : You don't want to be a tomboy anymore? Then add some **ruffles** to your wardrobe.

A : 我想買新衣服。

B : 再也不想穿得像男人婆了？那就買點有花邊的衣裳吧！

單字

wardrobe
[ˋwɔrd͵rob] n.
衣櫥；個人全部的
衣物

ruffle [ˋrʌfl] n.
（皺）褶飾；花邊；
荷葉邊

一窺時尚女子的衣櫥

tanktop 女用背心／吊帶

trench coat 軍式風衣

middy blouse 水手衫

knickerbockers 燈籠褲

puff sleeve 泡泡袖

tight 緊身衣

barrel skirt 直筒裙

waist high skirt 高腰裙

anorak （帶有帽子的）防風夾克

polo neck 高圓翻領衫

tight jeans 緊身牛仔褲

bootcut jeans 靴形牛仔褲

blazer 寬鬆的運動外套；印有校名的運動外衣

今晚打扮得漂亮點。

這句可以這麼說

Dress yourself up tonight.

Dress smartly tonight.

*Spruce yourself **up** tonight.

Wear your best **outfit** tonight.

學學老外這麼說

A : I've got two tickets for a concert. Wear your best outfit tonight.

B : I'd love to go. But sorry, I am otherwise engaged tonight.

A : 我買了兩張音樂會門票，晚上你要打扮漂亮一點。

B : 我很想去。但是今晚不行，對不起。

---

* spruce [sprus] v. 打扮。用法常為 spruce somebody / something / your-self up。

單字

outfit [`aʊt.fɪt] n.
全套服裝（尤指在特殊場合穿的）

The Secret of Women's No to Dates

1. I think of you as a brother. (You remind me of every banjo-playing geek on "Hee Haw.")
2. There's a slight difference in our ages. (You are one Jurassic geezer.)
3. I'm not attracted to you in that way. (You are the ugliest dork I have ever laid eyes upon.)
4. I've got a boyfriend. (I'd rather stay home alone.)
5. I don't date men where I work. (Hey, bud, I wouldn't even date you if you were in the same solar system, much less the same building.)
6. I'm concentrating on my career. (Even something as boring and as my job has got to be better than dating you.)
7. I'm celibate. (One look at you and I'm ready to swear off men altogether.)
8. Let's be friends. (I want you to stay around so I can tell you in excruciating detail about all the other men I meet and fall in love with.)

女人拒絕跟你約會的內幕

1. 我把你當弟弟看待。（你讓我想起「驢叫」電視節目上那些彈班卓琴的呆子。）
2. 我們的年齡差距有點大。（你根本是侏羅紀時代的老頭。）
3. 我對你沒有感覺。（你是我所見過最醜的傢伙。）
4. 我有男朋友了。（我寧願在家裡宅著。）
5. 我不談辦公室戀愛。（嘿，哥們，就算我們在同一個太陽系中我也不會和你約會的，在同一層樓就更不會了。）
6. 我現在心思全在工作上。（即使我的工作再無聊，也比你強。）
7. 我不打算結婚。（看你一眼，我已經準備發誓遠離男人。）
8. 我們做朋友吧！（我想讓你待在我的身旁，這樣我可以把我認識的、愛上的所有男人的細節告訴你折磨你。）

舞會有什麼穿著要求嗎？

這句可以這麼說

What's the *dress code for the party?

Is the party formal or casual?

What should I wear for the party?

學學老外這麼說

A : What's the dress code for the party?

B : Formal. Wear a suit and tie.

A : 舞會有什麼穿著要求嗎？

B : 正式。所以你得穿西裝、打領帶。

---

* dress code 穿著要求。

時尚情報站

歐美晚會宴會的「穿著要求（dress code）」很重要，如果衣著隨便，那麼在一群燕尾服和晚禮服裙中，就會引人側目。那麼穿著要求有哪幾類呢？

1. White tie / Ultra－formal 很正式，男士要穿燕尾服（tailcoat），女士要穿大裙襬的長晚禮服。

2. Black tie / Formal 正式，男士要穿晚禮服（tuxedo），女士要穿晚禮服（evening gown）。

3. Black tie optional / Creative black tie 要求較不嚴，正式服裝就可以。

4. Semi-formal 半正式，男士要穿深色西服，女士要穿短禮服或套裝。

5. Cocktail 雞尾酒會，半正式服裝就可以。

6. Smart casual 講究一點的便服。

7. Business casual 便裝，但禁穿牛仔褲。

8. Casual / informal 便裝，但禁穿短褲和拖鞋。

02 配件

MP3 018

這頂黑色天鵝絨貝蕾帽很經典。

這句可以這麼說

This black **velvet beret** is a classic.

This black velvet beret is a **timeless** item.

This black velvet beret never goes out of style.

學學老外這麼說

A : This black velvet beret is a classic. It goes with both casual and formal clothing.

B : I thought it would only go well with more elegant clothing.

A : 這頂黑色天鵝絨貝蕾帽很經典。配休閒裝和正式服裝都行。

B : 我還以為只能配比較淑女的衣服。

單字

velvet [ˋvɛlvɪt] n. 天鵝絨

beret [bəˋre] n. （法）貝蕾帽

timeless [ˋtaɪmləs] adj. 不受時間影響的；永久的

這頂帽子是手工織的。

這句可以這麼說

This hat is hand made.

This hat is hand-**knit**.

This is a hand-knit hat.

學學老外這麼說

A : Your hat is very special.

B : It was hand-knit by my mom.

A : 你的帽子很特別。

B : 我媽織給我的。

B : 這頂叢林帽可能較適合。

單字

knit [nɪt] v.
編織；針織衣物

歐式婚紗風格

A-line / Princess: An A-line or princess line wedding dress hugs the waist, creates a slimmer waistline, and flatters the bust. It's good for both wider hips or narrower hips.

A字公主裙婚紗：A字公主裙婚紗在腰部收緊，塑造出苗條的腰際線並襯托胸部，寬窄臀皆宜。

Ballerina: A ballerina wedding dress is for romantic brides with slim-hipped figures and a full bust.

芭蕾舞裙婚紗：芭蕾舞裙婚紗適合浪漫，窄臀豐胸的新娘。

Column: A column wedding dress looks great on tall, willowy brides.

直通型婚紗：直通型婚紗適合高挑苗條的新娘。

Empire Line: An empire line wedding dress is for brides with a broad waist and a small bust. It also makes petite brides taller.

帝國裙式婚紗：帝國裙式婚紗適合平胸寬腰的新娘，身材嬌小的新娘穿上能顯高。

Mermaid: A mermaid wedding dress is perfect for curvy girls with balanced hip and bust measurements.

魚尾裙式婚紗：魚尾裙式婚紗配身材勻稱曲線玲瓏的新娘。

MP3
020

這種船形帽既不能遮陽，也不太保暖。

This type of ***garrison cap** is not good for blocking the sun or keeping warm.

This type of garrison cap neither blocks out the sun nor keeps you warm.

This type of garrison cap is more of an adornment than a really useful accessory.

學學老外這麼說

A : I need a hat for hiking.

B : How about this garrison cap?

A : This type of garrison cap neither blocks out the sun nor keeps you warm.

B : Then this ***bush hat** may suit you.

A : 我需要一頂健走用的帽子。

B : 這頂船形帽如何？

A : 這種船形帽既不能遮陽，也不太保暖。

B : 這頂叢林帽可能較適合。

---

* garrison [`gærəsṇ] n. 守備部隊。garrison cap 指「船形帽」。

* bush [buʃ] n. 灌木。bush hat 指「寬邊的叢林帽」。

帽子大全

beret 貝蕾帽

bonnet 貝殼式女帽

bowler hat 圓頂硬禮帽

broad-brimmed straw hat 寬邊草帽

cap 便帽；鴨舌帽

cowboy hat 牛仔帽

garrison cap 船形帽

hat 有帽沿的帽子

hood 斗篷風帽

top hat 高頂絲質禮帽

Panama hat 巴拿馬草帽

bush hat 叢林帽（與牛仔帽相似，常為迷彩色）

你喜歡什麼樣的圍巾？

這句可以這麼說

What type of scarf do you like?

What kind of scarf do you prefer?

學學老外這麼說

A : What type of scarf do you prefer?

B : All types. I wear wool, **cashmere**, and fur scarves in fall and winter. And silk scarves to go with my clothing in spring and summer.

A : How about **shawls** or **stoles**?

B : Of course. I have a timeless Burberry **plaid** cashmere shawl.

A : 你喜歡什麼樣的圍巾？

B : 都喜歡。秋冬我都圍羊毛圍巾、喀什米爾或皮草圍巾，春夏就用絲巾搭配衣服。

A : 那大披肩呢？

B : 當然，我有一條永遠不過時的 Burberry 喀什米爾格子披肩。

單字

cashmere
[`kæʃmɪr] n. 羊絨；
喀什米爾羊毛

shawl [ʃɔl] n. 披肩

stole [stol] n. 披肩

plaid [plæd] n.
方格圖案；方格布

MP3
022

你的圍巾花色真好看。

這句可以這麼說

The pattern on your scarf is beautiful.

I like the pattern of your scarf.

學學老外這麼說

A：Your scarf has a very unique and lovely pattern.

B：It's Russian handmade style.

A：你的圍巾花色很獨特，很可愛。

B：這是俄羅斯的手工樣式。

MP3
023

這條絲巾配這件女襯衫嗎？

這句可以這麼說

Will this silk scarf go well with this blouse?

Will this silk scarf match this blouse?

Does this silk scarf look good with this blouse?

Can I wear this silk scarf with this blouse?

學學老外這麼說

A：Will this scarf go well with my blouse?

B：Not really. The red *clashes with the green.

A：這條絲巾配我這件女襯衫嗎？

B：不太配。紅色和綠色不搭。

---

* clash with 與……犯沖；與……不相配。

我不知道怎麼圍圍巾才好看。

這句可以這麼說

I don't know how to tie a scarf fashionably.

I don't know how to wear a scarf.

Do you know some ways to wear a scarf elegantly?

學學老外這麼說

A：I don't know how to tie a scarf fashionably.

B：You can wear it as a **bandana**, a purse tie, a **headband**, or with a bracelet.

A：我不知道怎樣圍圍巾才好看？

B：你可以把它摺成對角圍在脖子上，也可以綁在包包上，可以作髮帶綁頭髮，還可以和手鐲一起戴在手上。

單字

bandana
[bæn`dænə] n.
花色鮮豔的印花大手帕

headband
[`hɛd͵bænd] n.
髮帶

圍巾的經典繫法

❶ classic drape 垂於胸前

❷ classic flip 圍巾一頭甩到背後

❸ ascot knot 寬領帶結

❹ faux bow 大蝴蝶結

❺ French twist 法國結

❻ European loop / slip knot / hacking knot 雙層環結

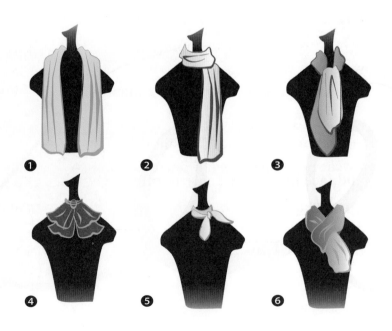

MP3
025

如何選擇適合臉型的墨鏡呢？

這句可以這麼說

How do you buy sunglasses that **flatter** your face?

How do you pick the perfect pair of sunglasses to suit the shape of your face?

How do you find the right sunglasses for your face?

What sunglasses will work with the shape of your face?

學學老外這麼說

A : What do I need to look for when choosing sunglasses for the shape of my face?

B : In general, you should choose a pair of shades in a shape that is the opposite of your face shape.

A : So a round face like mine can carry off **geometric** shapes, **ovals**, **wraps** and **shields**. Is that right?

B : Absolutely.

A : 如何選擇適合臉型的墨鏡呢？

B : 一般來說，你選的墨鏡鏡框要和你的臉型相反。

A : 那麼像我這樣圓臉的適合戴幾何圖形、橢圓的、寬版的或無框的。對嗎？

B : 非常正確。

單字

flatter [ˋflætɚ] v. 使（某人）顯得（較實際相貌）好看

geometric [dʒɪəˋmɛtrɪk] adj. 幾何線條；圖形的

oval [ˋovl] n. & adj. 橢圓形（的）

wrap [ræp] n. 寬版墨鏡（一般從眼角延伸至太陽穴）

shield [ʃild] n. 半框型或無框

防風眼鏡還沒過時呢！

這句可以這麼說

***Goggles** are still hot now.

Goggles are in now.

Goggles aren't out yet.

學學老外這麼說

A : I want to buy a pair of sunglasses. Are goggles still in now?

B : If I were you, I would pick the **aviator** glasses by **Ray Ban**. They are an all-time classic.

A : 我想買副墨鏡。防風眼鏡還流行嗎？

B : 是我的話，我就買雷朋的飛行員墨鏡，永遠是經典。

> 單字
>
> **aviator** [`evɪ.etɚ]
> n. 飛行員墨鏡（鏡片為水滴狀，鏡架為金屬）

---

* goggles [`ɡɑɡlz] n. 這個字除了指「防風眼鏡」外，也能指「蛙鏡」、「護目鏡」。

MP3
027

你戴這副墨鏡很有明星氣質。

這句可以這麼說

You've got the **charisma** of a star with those dark glasses.

You have the look of a movie star with those dark glasses.

You look like a movie star wearing those dark glasses.

學學老外這麼說

A : You've got the charisma of a star with those dark glasses.

B : Thanks.

A : 你戴這副墨鏡很有明星氣質。

B : 謝謝。

單字

charisma
[kə`rɪzmə] n. 氣質

墨鏡常識

Lenses 鏡片類型：

mirrored 反射（鏡面）　　　　　gradient 漸層

polarized 偏光　　　　　　　　photochromic 變色

tinted 有色

Style 鏡框款式：

❶ wraps 寬版墨鏡

❷ goggles 大眼眶太陽眼鏡（蛙鏡）

❸ shields 無框眼鏡

❹ aviators 飛行鏡（鏡片為水滴狀，金屬邊）

❺ clip-ons 夾鏡（方便附在普通眼鏡上的類型）

MP3
028

你喜歡什麼牌子的包包？

這句可以這麼說

What are your favorite brands of handbags?

What brands of handbags do you prefer?

What brands of handbags do you find attractive?

Do you have a preference for certain brands of handbags?

學學老外這麼說

A : What are your favorite brands of handbags?

B : Louis Vuitton, Prada, Coach, and Hermes.

A : Sorry, but I can only afford **replicas** of designer handbags.

A：你喜歡什麼牌子的包包？

B：LV、Prada、Coach或者愛馬仕。

A：對不起，我最多只能買得起名牌的A貨。

單字

replica [ˋrɛplɪkə] n. 複製品

43

MP3
029

我包包上的拉鍊壞了。

這句可以這麼說

I broke the **zipper** on my handbag.

The zipper on my handbag is **damaged**.

The zipper on my handbag doesn't work.

I need to have the zipper on my handbag fixed.

學學老外這麼說

A : The zipper on my handbag doesn't work.

B : A designer bag like this shouldn't be so easily damaged.

A : It's a *knock-off.

A : 我包包上的拉鍊壞了。

B : 名牌包不應該這麼快壞啊。

A : 這是A貨啦。

---

* knock-off 也寫作 knockoff，意指「仿製品」。

單字

zipper [ˋzɪpɚ] n. 拉鍊

damage [ˋdæmɪdʒ] v. 損壞；衣服配飾如標有 damaged，則為瑕疵品

這種包包實用嗎？

Is this handbag practical?

Is this handbag good for practical use?

A : Can I use this handbag on different occasions?

B : Yes. It's a very practical bag.

A : 我能在不同場合用這個包包嗎？

B : 是的，這是一款很實用的包包。

包包總動員

不同包包對應不同性格，你背的包包會說出你的性格哦！

如果有人問你：What type of handbags do you prefer? 你的回答可要謹慎了。

❶ briefcase 公事包──工作狂型

❷ evening bag 晚宴包──時尚舞會女皇型

❸ messenger bag 郵差包──隨興休閒型

❹ clutch bag 手拿包──自信幹練型

❺ diaper bag 媽咪包──顧家型

❻ eco-friendly tote 環保托特包──環保主義型

❼ backpack 雙肩背包──休閒健康型

❽ oversized bag 超大肩包──時尚忙碌型

❾ shoulder bag 單肩包──敏感實際型

❿ wristlet 手腕包──工作型

031

這香水是柑橘味道。

This perfume smells like **citrus**.

This perfume is citrus flavored.

This is a citrus perfume.

A : Excuse me. What perfume *scent is this?

B : This is a citrus perfume. Would you like to try it?

A : 對不起。這香水是什麼味道的？

B : 這香水是柑橘味道。你要試試嗎？

單字

citrus [ˋsɪtrəs] n. adj. 柑橘；柑橘屬植物的

---

* scent [sɛnt] n. 香味；氣味。

47

香水要噴在脈搏點。

這句可以這麼說

Wear perfume on your *pulse points.

Spray perfume on your pulse points.

Apply perfume to your pulse points.

學學老外這麼說

A : How do you wear perfume?

B : Apply perfume to your pulse points, the **crook** of the elbow, the back of the knees, cleavage, and neck.

A : 怎麼噴香水啊?

B : 可以噴在脈搏點、肘窩、膝間、胸前和脖子上。

單字

spray [spre] v. 噴

apply [ə`plaɪ] v. 塗抹

crook [krʊk] n. 彎曲;彎曲處

---

* pulse [pʌls] n. 脈搏。

MP3
033

這家鞋店在清倉大拍賣。

━━━ 這句可以這麼說 ━━━

The shoes in this store are on sale.

This shoe store is having a huge sale.

This shoe store is having a *clearance sale.

The poster of this shoe store says *everything must go!

━━━ 學學老外這麼說 ━━━

A : Giordano is having a clearance sale.

B : Yes. The poster says everything must go!

A : *Clearance items only. New lines are not included.

A : 佐丹奴在清倉大拍賣。

B : 是呀，海報上寫說一件不留呢！

A : 僅限清倉貨和零碼商品，新品不包括在內。

────────────

* clearance sale 清倉大拍賣。

* clearance item 清倉貨；零碼。

* everything must go 一件不留。

A Crowded Shoe Store

It was the day of the big sale. Rumors of the sale (and some advertising in the local paper) were the main reason for the long line that formed in front of the store by 8:30, the shoe store`s opening time.

A small man pushed his way to the front of the line, only to be pushed back, amid loud and colorful curses. On the man's second attempt, he was punched square in the jaw and knocked around a bit. Then he was thrown to the end of the line again. As he got up a second time, he said to the person at the end of the line...

"That does it! If they hit me one more time, I won't open the store!"

擁擠的鞋店

拍賣當天，口耳相傳的威力加上當地報紙廣告影響，該鞋店在 8:30 開門之前，門口就已經大排長龍。

一個矮小的男人使勁擠到前面，又被推了回來，人群中喧鬧聲不斷，還夾著叫罵聲。那名男子又試了一次，結果下巴挨了一拳，又被推了出來，被扔到隊尾。第二次他站起來的時候，對後面的人說：「夠了！如果你們再揍我，我就不開門了！」

The Big Sale

MP3
034

我要找一雙黑色皮革的楔型鞋。

(Shoes)

I'm looking for a pair of black *wedge-heeled leather shoes.

Have you got a pair of black wedge-heeled leather shoes?

I'd like a pair of black wedge-heeled leather shoes.

Where can I find black wedge-heeled leather shoes?

A : I'm looking for a pair of black wedge-heeled leather shoes.

B : How about this pair? *Patent leather shoes are really in now.

A : But they **scuff** easily.

A : 我想找一雙黑色皮革的楔型鞋。

B : 這雙怎樣？漆皮現在很流行。

A : 但是漆皮鞋很容易磨損。

單字

scuff [skʌf] v.
磨出痕跡來

---

* wedge-heels 楔型鞋。
* patent leather 漆皮。

皮鞋料面面觀

patent leather 漆皮

metallic leather 金屬感皮面

suede 仿麂皮

pebbled leather 荔枝紋皮面

mirrored leather 亮面皮

calf leather 小牛皮

goatskin 羊皮

artificial leather 人造皮革

鞋子：美麗與健康

stiletto 細高跟鞋	會造成	bunion 拇指囊炎
pointy-toe shoes 尖頭鞋	會造成	callus 硬皮；長繭 corn 雞眼 hammertoe 槌狀趾；腳趾關節彎曲 sprain one's ankle 扭傷腳踝
flat 平跟鞋	會造成	arch and Achilles tendon problems 足弓和阿基里斯腱的問題
platform shoes 厚底鞋	會造成	sprain one's ankle 扭傷腳踝
mules（拖鞋式）休閒鞋 flip-flops 人字拖	會造成	slips 滑倒

比起中跟鞋，我更喜歡細高跟。

這句可以這麼說

I prefer **stilettos** to *****kitten heels**.

I'm definitely a fan of stilettos, not kitten heels.

I've set my heart on stilettos rather than kitten heels.

學學老外這麼說

A : Nearly all your shoes are high heels!

B : I just love them more than anything.

A : 你幾乎所有的鞋都是高跟的！

B : 我很喜歡它們啊！

單字
stiletto [stɪˋlɛto] n.
（口）細高跟女鞋

---

* kitten heels 中跟鞋。

合腳嗎？

這句可以這麼說

How do they fit?

Do they fit all right?

How do they feel?

學學老外這麼說

A : How do they feel?

B : I am afraid they are a bit tight. They **pinch**.

A : 合腳嗎？

B : 我覺得太緊了，很夾腳。

單字

pinch [pɪntʃ] v.
夾腳；掐痛；擠痛

穿這雙鞋腳後跟會痛。

這句可以這麼說

They hurt at the heel.

Those shoes pinch me at the heel.

They are too tight on the heel.

My heels hurt when I walk in these shoes.

學學老外這麼說

A : My heels hurt when I walk in this new pair of
   leather shoes.

B : Stuff them with wet newspaper and leave them for 3
   days. It always works.

A : Thank you!

A : 穿這雙新皮鞋腳後跟有點痛。

B : 在裡面塞滿溼報紙，放三天，就會很好穿。

A : 謝謝！

其他鞋類

❶ sandals 涼鞋

❷ slippers 室內用的便鞋／拖鞋

❸ kitten heels 中跟鞋

❹ Mary Janes 娃娃鞋；瑪莉珍繫帶鞋

❺ pumps （無扣、無帶的）高跟鞋

❻ ballet flats 圓頭平底鞋

❼ snow boots 雪靴

❽ wedge-qwheels 楔型鞋

03 珠寶首飾

MP3
038

我們去珠寶店逛逛吧。

這句可以這麼說

Let's have a look at that jewelry store.

Let's go look in the jewelry store.

Would you like to look around in the jewelry store?

學學老外這麼說

A : Tiffany has launched some new **collections**. Let's go look for it.

B : You can just visit its website. It would be much easier.

A : But that's a totally different **feel**.

A : 蒂芬尼推出了一系列新作。想和我去看看嗎？

B : 你看它的網站就好啦，比較簡單一點。

A : 感覺不一樣啦。

單字

collection
[kə`lɛkʃən] n.
一系列產品；收藏品

feel [fɪl] n.
（環境等給人的）
感覺

57

Dumb Beast

Watching her mother as she tried on her new fur coat, Becky said unhappily, "Mom, do you realize some poor dumb beast suffered so you could have that?" The woman shot her an angry look, "Becky, how dare you talk about your father like that!"

無言的動物

看著媽媽試穿新買的毛皮大衣，貝琪很不高興地說：「媽媽，你有沒有想過為了這件衣服，有多少可憐的動物遭受痛苦？」

她媽媽很生氣地瞪了她一眼，「貝琪，你怎麼敢這麼說你爸！」

*註：dumb 有「說不出話的；啞的；愚笨的」意思。

MP3 039

這條項鍊是純金的嗎？

這句可以這麼說

Is this necklace pure gold?
Is this necklace 24 **karat** gold?
What's the ***purity** of this gold necklace?

學學老外這麼說

A : This necklace is gorgeous. Is it pure gold?
B : It's 18-karat gold. It's harder and more durable.
A : 這條項鍊好漂亮。它是純金的嗎？
B : 18K 金的。它比純金更硬，更持久。

單字
karat [ˋkærət] n.
開（黃金純度單位）

* purity [ˋpjurətɪ] n. 原意為「純淨」，這裡則有「純度」的意思。

MP3
040

這個網站 14K 金的金飾打對折（買一送一）。

You can get 50% off on a 14 karat **charm** on this website.

If you buy one 14 karat charm on this website, you get one free.

A : Is it safe to buy jewelry on the Internet?
B : It depends. Why?
A : This website is offering "*buy one and get one free" deals. I love these **bangles**.

A : 在網路上買首飾安全嗎？
B : 看情況。怎麼了？
A : 這個網站在辦「買一送一」的活動，我滿喜歡這些鐲子的。

單字

charm [tʃɑrm] n.
（手鐲等上頭的）
吉祥小飾品

bangle [ˋbæŋgl]
n. 手鐲；腳鍊（一般也稱 bracelet 手鐲；anklet 腳鍊）

---

* buy one get one free 買一送一。

戴純銀首飾能去風溼。

這句可以這麼說

***Fine silver** jewelry can cure **rheumatism**.

Fine silver jewelry can treat rheumatism.

學學老外這麼說

A : Your silver bracelet is **tarnished**.

B : Yes, I need to clean it. I guess it's treating my rheumatism.

A : Really? As far as I know, it's due to exposure to **humidity**.

A : 你的銀手鐲都發黑了。

B : 是該清洗了。我想它正在去我的風溼病。

A : 是嗎？就我所知，是因為受潮了。

單字

rheumatism
[ˈrumə.tɪzəm] n.
風溼病

tarnish [ˈtɑrnɪʃ] v.
失去光澤

humidity
[hjuˈmɪdətɪ] n. 溼氣

---

* fine silver 純銀

這個銀項圈是祖傳的。

這句可以這麼說

This silver **neckband** is an **heirloom**.

I ***inherited** this silver neckband from my great grandmother.

This is an heirloom silver neckband from my great grandmother.

學學老外這麼說

A : What a cool silver neckband!

B : I inherited it from my great grandmother.

A : No wonder the carved pattern is so **ornate** and special.

A : 好酷的銀項圈！

B : 我的曾祖母傳給我的。

A : 難怪雕刻的圖案這麼華麗、特別。

單字

neckband
[ˋnɛkˏbænd] n. 項圈

heirloom [ˋɛrˏlum]
n.（貴重的）祖傳遺
物；傳家寶

ornate [ɔrˋnet] adj.
華麗的

---

* inherit [ɪnˋhɛrɪt] v. 繼承。

金銀首飾小常識

金飾不再是單一的金黃色，合金的出現讓時尚多了更多的選擇，金飾以黃金含量來分級，最純的為 24K，然後依次是 22K，18K，14K，12K，10K，在美國 10K 是金飾的最低級別。現在，訂婚戒指最常用的是 14K 金的。看看不同的合金：

white gold 白金

green gold 綠金

rose gold 玫瑰金

mosaic gold 彩金

另外還有鍍金（gold plated）和（鉑金 platinum），千萬不要把 platinum 和 white gold 搞混了，真正的鉑金飾都標有「pt」。

那銀首飾的純度又有什麼學問呢？

fine silver 999 純銀

sterling silver 925 純銀

coin silver 800 或 900 銀

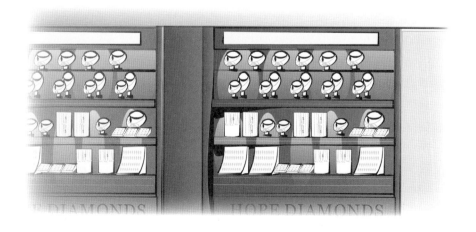

MP3
043

這款珍珠項鍊真精緻。

這句可以這麼說

How elegant this pearl necklace is!

This pearl necklace is so fine.

This pearl necklace feels fantastic.

This pearl necklace makes me *feel like a million dollars.

學學老外這麼說

A : This pearl necklace feels like a million dollars.

B : Yeah, it's so elegant. It will look good with your black velvet **evening gown**.

A : 這個珍珠項鍊真精緻。

B : 是啊，很高貴。戴在你的黑色天鵝絨晚禮服上肯定很漂亮。

單字

evening gown
[`ìvnɪŋ `gaʊn] n.
（女性的）晚禮服

---

* feel like a million dollars 字面意思是「像一百萬美元」，用來形容「好得不能再好」的心情或狀況。

我喜歡耳針式的珍珠耳環，而不是誇張的圈圈耳環。

這句可以這麼說

I love *posts with small pearls better than showy large *hoop earrings.

I like *studs set with small pearls. Large hoop earrings are too flashy.

I prefer small pearl stud earrings to fancy large hoop earrings.

學學老外這麼說

A : Look, I've bought you a new pair of earrings.

B : Thank you. I love these studs set with small pearls. Large hoop earrings are too flashy.

A：我買了對新耳環給你。

B：謝謝。我喜歡這種耳針式的珍珠耳環，（因為）圈圈耳環太誇張了。

---

* posts [posz] 和 studs [stʌdz] 在這裡均指「耳針式耳環」。

* hoop earrings 圈圈耳環。（dangling earrings 吊墜耳環）

這是真的嗎？

Is it *genuine?

Is this real?

A : Is this a real string of pearls?

B : You can return if it is fake. We have a "30-day unconditional *return policy".

A : 這串珍珠是真的嗎？

B : 如果是假的你可退貨。我們有「三十天鑑賞期」的規定。

---

* genuine ['dʒɛnjuɪn] adj. 真的；誠實可靠的。

* return policy 退貨政策。

首飾的材料

precious metals 貴重金屬：gold 金；silver 銀；platinum 鉑金

other metals 其他金屬：stainless steel 不鏽鋼；copper 銅；brass 黃銅；titanium 鈦

precious gems、stones & crystals 寶石、石頭和水晶：diamonds 鑽石；rubies 紅寶石；sapphires 藍寶石

other gems、stones & crystals 其他寶石、石頭和水晶：agate 瑪瑙；tiger eye 虎眼石；zircon 鋯石

animal origin 來自於動物：hair 毛髮；bone 骨頭；leather 皮革；feathers 羽毛；wool 羊毛

plant origin 來自於植物：wood 木頭；seeds 種子；bark 樹皮；hemp 大麻；string 植物纖維；flowers 花

ocean origin 來自於海洋：coral 珊瑚；shells 貝殼；pearls 珍珠；bone 骨頭

manufactured materials 人造材料：ceramics 瓷；glass 玻璃；plastics 塑膠；rubbers 橡膠

MP3
046

買鑽石要注意什麼？

這句可以這麼說

What's the best way to buy a diamond?

How does one shop for a diamond?

Do you have any tips on diamond shopping?

Can you give me any tips on buying a diamond?

學學老外這麼說

A : I am going to propose to Harriet. How does one
shop for a diamond *engagement ring?

B : Select a reputable jeweler and choose a diamond
that carries a *GIA report.

A : 我要向哈莉特求婚。如何買訂婚鑽戒呢？

B : 找信譽好的珠寶店，買有美國珠寶學院權威檢測認證的鑽石。

---

* engagement ring 訂婚戒指。在西方訂婚戒指一般為鑽戒，婚後配戴「黃金戒
  指」（plain gold ring）。

* GIA The Gemological Institute of America 的縮寫，指國際權威的鑽石檢
  測機構─美國珠寶學院。

你有（寶石）鑑定書嗎？

這句可以這麼說

Does this come with a certificate of **authenticity**?

Can I get proof of **appraisal**?

Do you have anything certifying the authenticity of the ***gem**?

學學老外這麼說

A : Do you have anything certifying the authenticity of the diamond?

B : Yes, here is the GIA report.

A : 這顆鑽石有鑑定書嗎？

B : 有，這是美國珠寶學院的認證。

單字

authenticity
[ˌɔθɛnˋtɪsətɪ] n.
真實性

appraisal [əˋprezl]
n. 鑑定；評價

---

* gem [dʒɛm] n.（已切割打磨的）寶石。

The Cursed Diamond Ring

"Rachel, darling, how wonderful to see you after all these years! My God, what an incredibly large diamond ring you've got. Is it a famous diamond?"

"Oh yes, Hermione, it's the famous Bloomenstein diamond, but it's cursed."

"Really, what's the curse?"

"Mr. Bloomenstein, of course!" says Rachel.

被詛咒的鑽戒

「瑞秋，親愛的，過了這麼多年再見到你真高興！我的天哪，你的戒指大得令人不敢置信。是一顆名鑽嗎？」

「噢，是的，赫敏。它是著名的布魯門斯坦鑽石，但它受了詛咒。」

「真的嗎？是什麼詛咒？」

「當然是布魯門斯坦先生咒，我深受其苦。」瑞秋說。

這看起來像是假的。

這句可以這麼說

It looks fake.

It looks **phony**.

This doesn't look real.

It looks like an *imitation.

學學老外這麼說

A : I got this Cartier *brooch for only $10. What a **bargain**!

B : To tell you the truth, it looks like an imitation.

A : 我花了十美元買了這個卡地亞胸針，撿了個大便宜。

B : 說實話，這看起來像假的。

---

* imitation [ˌɪməˈteʃən] n. 仿冒品。

* brooch [brotʃ] n. 胸針；領針。

單字

phony [ˈfonɪ] a.
假冒的

bargain [ˈbɑrɡən]
n. 便宜貨

鑽石恆久遠，一顆永流傳

鑽石是永恆愛情的象徵，是珠寶首飾裡的皇后。要買到好的鑽石，首先要瞭解鑽石的四要素：克拉、顏色、淨度和切割（the 4 C's: carat, color, clarity, and cut.）

1.「克拉（carat）」不用解釋大家都知道，克拉數越大越有價值。如果詢問克拉數，可說：How many carats is this?

2.「顏色（color）」，物以稀為貴，女士們肯定記得電影「色戒」中的鴿子蛋「粉鑽（pink diamond）」和「黃鑽（yellow diamond）」，還有李奧納多演的電影「血鑽石（Blood Diamond）」。另外還有聞名世界的「希望之星（The Hope Diamond）」是一顆「藍鑽（blue diamond）」。

3.「淨度（clarity）」，只有高倍放大鏡才能看出雜質。high clarity 指鑽石淨度高，low clarity 當然是淨度低了。一般淨度等級 從 FL（完美無瑕）到 IF（內部完美無瑕）至 I（有瑕疵）排列不等。

4.「切割（cut）」，well cut 指切割優良，poor cut 指的就是切工不好。目前 brilliant cut 明亮式切割，是最閃爍最具亮度的切割方式。

水鑽和鑽石一樣閃亮，但便宜多了。

這句可以這麼說

*Cz diamonds** are just as brilliant as diamonds, but much cheaper.

Cz diamonds can compete with diamonds in brilliancy but are much cheaper.

Cz diamonds almost equal diamonds in brilliancy but sell for a much lower price.

學學老外這麼說

A : I wanna buy my girlfriend a birthday gift. Any suggestions?

B : How about cz diamond jewelry? They look just as brilliant as diamonds, but are much cheaper.

A : 我要給我女朋友買生日禮物。有什麼建議嗎？

B : 水鑽首飾如何？水鑽和鑽石一樣閃亮，但便宜多了。

---

* cz diamond 指「水鑽」，cz 為 Cubic Zirconium（方晶鋯石）的縮略。

Top 10 Jewelry Brands 十大珠寶品牌

1. Harry Winston 海瑞溫斯頓

2. Buccellati 布契拉提

3. Enzo 勞倫斯

4. Tiffany & Co. 蒂芬尼

5. Cartier 卡地亞

6. Bulgari 寶格麗

7. Tasaki 田崎珠寶

8. Mikimoto 御木本

9. Graff 格拉夫

10. Chopard 蕭邦

小笑話一則

Proposal

An enormously wealthy 65-year-old man falls in love with a young woman in her twenties and is contemplating a proposal.

"Do you think she'll marry me if I tell her I'm 45?" he asked a friend.

"Your chances are better," said the friend, "if you tell her you're 90."

求婚

有個六十五歲的大富翁愛上了一個二十多歲的年輕姑娘。他想向她求婚。

「你覺得如果我告訴她，我今年四十五歲，她會嫁給我嗎？」他問他的朋友。

「如果你告訴她，你已經九十歲了，」他的朋友說：「成功的機會更大。」

MP3
050

簡單的水鑽款式適合你活潑的性格。

Simple type of cz diamonds matches your active personality perfectly.

Simple type of cz diamonds is just right for athletic girls like you.

Simple type of cz diamonds wouldn't interfere with your outgoing personality.

學學老外這麼說

A : What type of cz diamonds look good on me?

B : Large glittering cz diamonds are for **trendsetters**. Curving lines, old-fashioned and intricate patterns are romantic. And those simple ones would match your active personality perfectly.

A : 哪種水鑽適合我呢？

B : 大而亮的適合引領潮流的女生。富有曲線，老式而華麗的款式比較 浪漫。那些簡單的水鑽款式才適合你活潑的性格。

單字

trendsetter
[`trɛnd͵sɛtɚ] n.
引領潮流的人

75

What's your birthstone? （你的生日石是什麼？）

January: Garnet　（一月：石榴石 ）

February:Amethyst（二月：紫水晶 ）

March:Aquamarine（三月：海藍寶石）

April:Diamond（四月：鑽石 ）

May: Emerald（五月：綠寶石）

June: Pearl and Alexandrite（六月：珍珠和紫翠玉）

July: Ruby（七月：紅寶石）

August: Peridot（八月：翠綠橄欖石 ）

September: Sapphire（九月：藍寶石）

October: Tourmaline and Opal（十月：電氣石和蛋白石）

November: Topaz and Citrine（十一月：黃玉〔拓帕石〕和黃水晶）

December: Tanzanite, Zircon, and Turquoise（十二月：丹泉石、鋯石和綠松石）

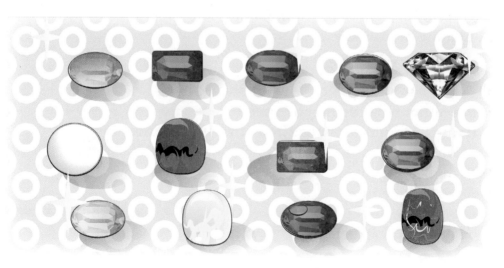

04 愛車

MP3
051

新手應該先買二手車練習。

這句可以這麼說

It is better for a new driver to buy a used car for practice.

A new driver should buy a second-hand car to practice with.

Buying pre-owned cars is more practical for a ***novice** driver.

學學老外這麼說

A : Should a new driver like me buy a second-hand car to practice with?

B : Not necessarily. You will drive more carefully with a new car.

A : 像我這樣的新手是不是應該買二手車練習？

B : 不必非如此不可，開新車你會更小心。

---

* novice [`nɑvɪs] n. 新手，初學者。

你打算買小型車嗎？

這句可以這麼說

Are you going to buy an economy car with a small engine?

Will you buy a small car with a small engine?

Will you choose an economy car with a small engine?

Have you set your mind on an economy car with a small engine?

學學老外這麼說

A：Will you choose an economy car with a small engine?

B：Definitely. Gas prices keep going up.

A：你打算買小型車嗎？

B：沒錯，油價一直在漲。

車型大全

MINI
迷你型

ECONOMY
經濟型

COMPACT
小型

INTERMEDIAT
中型

STANDARD
標準型

FULL-SIZE
全尺寸型

PREMIUM
高端型

LUXURY
豪華型

CONVERTIBLE
敞篷車

SPORTS CAR
跑車

MINIVAN
小型旅行車

SPORT UTILITY
全尺寸旅行車；休旅車

FULL SIZE VAN
運動型多功能車

PICK-UP TRUCK
輕型小貨車

我的車裝了衛星導航。

這句可以這麼說

I have a ***GPS** system in my car.

I installed a GPS ***device** in my car.

My car has GPS.

學學老外這麼說

A : Did you install a GPS device in your car?

B : Not yet. I want to buy a multifunctional one that can also serve as a TV, MP5, camera, phone, and Internet connection.

A : 你的車裝衛星導航了嗎？

B : 還沒。我想買一個多功能的，要能看電視、聽音樂、照相、打電話和上網。

---

* GPS Global Positioning System 全球定位系統

* device [dɪˈvaɪs] n. 裝置，儀器；炸彈。

MP3
054

哪裡能停車？

這句可以這麼說

Where can I park?

Where can I find a parking space?

Is there a parking lot nearby?

學學老外這麼說

A : Excuse me, where can I park?

B : There is an underground parking lot around the
corner.

A : 請問一下，哪裡能停車？

B : 街角有個地下停車場。

MP3
055

新手上路！請保持距離！

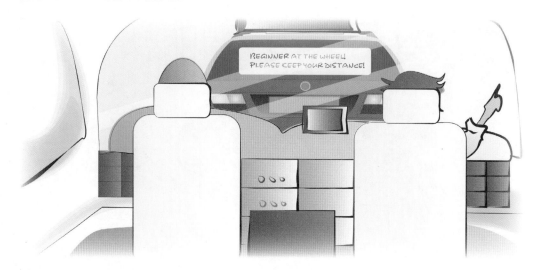

這句可以這麼說

Beginner at the wheel! Please keep your distance!

*Newbie driver! Please keep your distance!

New driver! Please maintain a safe distance!

New driver! Please keep clear!

學學老外這麼說

A : *Look out for that car!

B : What's wrong?

A : It says "Beginner at the wheel! Please keep your distance!"

A : 小心那輛車。

B : 怎麼了？

A : 它貼著「新手上路！請保持距離！」的牌子。

---

* newbie ['nubɪ] n. 新手（常用來指剛開始學習操作電腦者）。

* look out / watch out 小心。

你知道好的修車廠嗎？

這句可以這麼說

You know any good *garages?

Can you recommend an auto repair shop for me?

How can I find a good auto mechanic?

學學老外這麼說

A : You know any good garages? I want to replace my manual transmission with an automatic one.

B : Matrix Car Repair is not bad.

A : 你知道好的修車廠嗎？我想把我的手排改成自排的。

B : 美傑仕修車廠不錯。

---

* garages [gəˈrɑʒ] n. 修車廠；車庫 v. 把車送修。

MP3
057

我的車發動不起來。

這句可以這麼說

I can't start my car.

My car won't start.

學學老外這麼說

A：Shoot! My car won't start.

B：Let me help you.

A：真糟糕！我的車發動不起來。

B：我來幫你。

MP3
058

我的車引擎故障了。

My car has broken down.
The engine *cut out.
My engine isn't working.

A : My engine cut out.
B : Let me have a look.

A : 我的車引擎故障了。
B : 我來檢查一下。

---

* cut out 壞掉了,故障。

小笑話一則

Water in the Carburetor

Wife: "There's trouble with the car. It has water in the carburetor."
Husband: "Water in the carburetor? That's ridiculous."
Wife: "I tell you, the car has water in the carburetor."
Husband: "You don't even know what a carburetor is. Wher's the car?"
Wife: "In the swimming pool."

汽化器進水了

妻子：「汽車出問題了。汽化器裡進水了。」
丈夫：「汽化器裡進水了？真可笑！」
妻子：「我告訴你，汽化器裡進水了！」
丈夫：「你哪知道什麼是汽化器。車在哪？」
妻子：「在游泳池裡。」

我的車有一個輪胎爆胎了。

Dr 1234

這句可以這麼說

I have a **flat** *tyre.

One of my tires was **punctured**.

One of my tires blew out.

學學老外這麼說

A : One tire is flat.

B : Then we cannot drive on it.

A : 我的車有一個輪胎爆胎了。

B : 那就不能開了。

---

* tyre [taɪr] n. 輪胎。tyre 為英式用法，美式用法則寫作「tire」。

我車子的保險桿漆被人刮了一塊。

這句可以這麼說

Somebody **chipped** the paint on the bumper of my car.
Somebody chipped some paint off my bumper.
The paint on the bumper is **scratched**.

學學老外這麼說

A : Somebody chipped some paint off my bumper.

B : What rotten luck!

A : 我車子的保險桿漆被人刮了一塊。

B : 真倒楣！

單字

chip [tʃɪp] v.
剝落；刮落；蹭落漆片

scratch [skrætʃ] v.
刮；劃出傷痕

MP3
061

車子乾洗會傷車漆嗎？

這句可以這麼說

Will a dry car wash damage the paint?

Will a dry car wash do *harm to the paint?

Will a dry car wash scratch the paint?

學學老外這麼說

A : Will a dry car wash damage the paint?

B : I don't think so. It's also environmentally friendly.

A : 車子乾洗會傷車漆嗎？

B : 我不這麼認為，它很環保呢！

---

* harm [harm] n. & v. 損害。

062

我車子的方向燈壞了。

The turn signal of my car is broken.

The turn signal of my car isn't working.

The turn signal of my car is *__on the fritz__.

學學老外這麼說

A：The turn signal of my car isn't working.

B：You need to replace your turn signal **relay**.

A：我車子的方向燈壞了。

B：你得換個方向燈繼電器。

單字

relay [rɪ`le] n.
繼電器

---

* fritz [frɪts] n. 這個字指「德國兵」，帶有貶意，on the fritz 為美式用法，意為
「故障」。

汽車部位簡介

❶ windshield 擋風玻璃　　　❷ hood 引擎蓋 （美國：bonnet）

❸ bumper 保險桿　　　❹ door 車門

❺ hubcap 轂蓋　　　❻ tire 輪胎

❼ headlight 前燈　　　❽ turn signal 方向燈

❾ license plate 車牌

❿ side mirror 照後鏡（車內的後視鏡則為rear view mirror）

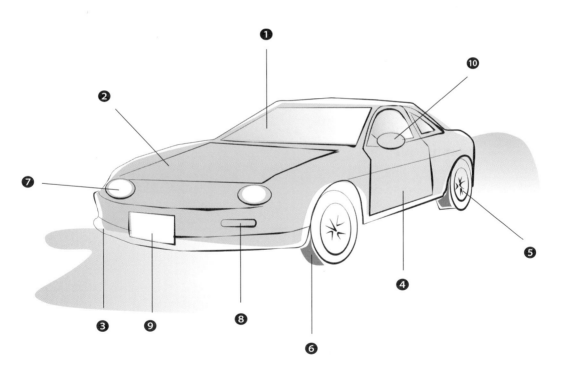

MP3 063

請加滿油！

Please fill up the **tank**.

****Top up** the tank, please!

Fill 'er up!

Please fill it up.

A : Top up the tank, please!

B : Sorry. This is a ***self-service** gas station.

A：請加滿油！

B：對不起，這裡是自助加油站。

---

* top up 加滿，把容器填滿。

* self-served 自助的。

單字

tank [tæŋk] n. 油箱

有沒有省油的好方法？

這句可以這麼說

Do you know how to save gas?

Do you have any *fuel economy tips?

Do you have any fuel efficiency tips?

Do you know any green driving techniques?

學學老外這麼說

A : My gas bill is beyond my budget. Do you have any fuel efficiency tips?

B : Just drive less and plan your trips in advance.

A : 我的油費超支了。有沒有省油的好方法？

B : 少開車，開車前先計畫好怎麼走。

---

* fuel [`fjuəl] n. 燃料　v.（為汽車等交通工具）加油。

定期保養你的車。

這句可以這麼說

Your car needs regularly scheduled maintenance.

I suggest regular maintenance for your car.

Regular car care is very important.

Give your car a ***tune up** regularly.

學學老外這麼說

A：How can I save on gas?

B：Give your car a tune up regularly.

A：怎麼省油啊？

B：定期保養你的車。

---

* tune up 原指樂器調音，此處指保養車。

我們共乘上班吧,可以節省油錢。

這句可以這麼說

Let's ***car-pool** to work, so we can save on gas.

Do you mind car-pooling? I can pay you on gas.

Would you like to car-pool with me? We can split the gas.

學學老外這麼說

A : Let's car-pool to work, so we can save on gas.

B : Are there any other car-poolers? I am worried about their car-pooling *etiquette.

A : 我們共乘上班吧,可以省油錢。

B : 還有其他共乘的人嗎?我擔心他們缺乏基本的共乘禮節。

---

* car pool 共乘。

* etiquette [`ɛtɪ͵kɛt] n. 禮儀,規矩。

省油方法大會串

1. Drive less. （少開車。）

2. Find good prices. （找個低油價的地方。）除了上網詢價，還要注意：
   · Determine whether gas with **ethanol** is right for your vehicle. （看看你的車能不能用加乙醇的汽油。）
   · Don't refill your tank until the last quarter tank, but don't push it any further. （直到剩四分之一再加油，但也不要剩太少才加。）
   · Fill the tank, but don't top it off. （加油一定要加滿，但別加多了。）

3. Take care of your car. （保養車子）。包括定期保養、換好的輪胎和空氣過濾器（air filter）等等。

4. Buy a different car, such as a **diesel**, **hybrid**, or smaller car. （換輛車，比如柴油車、混合動力車或小型車。）

5. Drive smarter.（開車有技巧。）
   · Avoid **idling**. （避免停車放空檔不熄火。）
   · Use a global positioning system.（使用 GPS 導航儀。）
   · Drive at a consistent speed.（定速行駛。）
   · Avoid stops and anticipate the stop signs and lights.（少停車，事先預測停車號誌和紅綠燈。）
   · Slow down.（開車慢行。）
   · Take off slowly from a full stop.（要慢慢發動熄火的車子。）
   · Shift into neutral if you are not comfortable with **downshifting**. （如果你不喜歡低檔，換中檔。）
   · Park in the shade. （在陰涼處停車。）

ethanol 乙醇	**disel** 柴油
hydrid 混合動力	**idle** 掛空檔
downshift 掛低檔	

容貌保養

不老並非神話，青春總是傳奇！時尚女子妙手回春，巧用瓶瓶罐罐抹平歲月痕跡，妙筆生花幻彩七十二色描出姹紫嫣紅：看她「膚細如瓷（porcelain-like skin）」、「明眸如星（radiant eyes）」、「光彩照人（glowing）」、「裸妝（nude look）」如清水出芙蓉、「晚妝（evening makeup）」如盛開花朵，好一個「濃妝淡抹總相宜」！祕密就在她的「化妝包（cosmetic bag）」裡，「保溼噴霧（hydrating spray）」、「粉底（foundation）」、「唇膏（lipstick）」加上「眉筆（eyebrow pencil）」……一應俱全，時時展現完美光彩！

MP3
067

你是乾性還是油性膚質？

這句可以這麼說

Do you have oily or dry skin?

Is your skin oily or dry?

What kind of skin do you have, oily or dry?

學學老外這麼說

A：What kind of skin do you have, oily or dry?

B：Normal.

A：你是油性還是乾性膚質？

B：中性膚質。

MP3
068

我是乾性和敏感型肌膚。

這句可以這麼說

My skin is dry and sensitive.
I have very dry and sensitive skin.

學學老外這麼說

A : My skin is sensitive and feels tight and dry *year-round.

B : It needs **hydration** and **nourishment**.

A：我的皮膚敏感，一整年都覺得緊繃又乾燥的。

B：你需要保溼和滋養。

單字

hydration
[haɪ`dreʃən] n.
水分；保溼

nourishment
[`nɝɪʃmənt] n. 營養

---

* year-round 一年到頭，整年。

MP3
069

我的皮膚粗糙、毛孔粗大。

這句可以這麼說

I have rough skin and enlarged **pores**.

My rough skin and large pores are bothering me.

學學老外這麼說

A : My skin is no longer smooth. Actually, my rough skin and large pores are really bothering me now.

B : What you need are quality **skincare** products and exercise.

A : 我的皮膚沒有以前光滑了。事實上，我最近一直為皮膚粗糙、毛孔粗大煩惱。

B : 你需要好的保養品和運動。

單 字

pore [por] n. 毛孔

skincare
[`skɪnˌkɛr] adj.
護膚的

皮膚類型

dry skin 乾性	oily skin 油性
normal skin 中性	sensitive skin 敏感性皮膚
combination skin 混合性皮膚	mature skin 老化皮膚
dull skin 暗沉皮膚	sun damaged skin 晒傷皮膚
enlarged pores 毛孔粗大	

小笑話一則

Breaking up

There was a pretty nurse named Carol who broke her engagement to a doctor. She was explaining everything to a friend.
"Do you mean to say," exclaimed Cindy, "that the bum asked you to give back the ring AND all his presents?"
"Not only that," said Carol, "he sent me a bill for 37 visits."

分手

有一個叫卡蘿的漂亮護士和一個醫生解除了婚約。她把一切事情說給她的朋友辛蒂聽。
「你是說，」辛蒂問，「那渾蛋要你把戒指還給他，還要討回所有的禮物？」
「不只這樣，」卡蘿說：「他還寄給我一張看三十七次病的帳單。」

MP3 070

你把皮膚晒得好漂亮！

這句可以這麼說

Nice *suntan!

What a nice, even tan!

You have a great **tan**!

Your skin is really nicely tanned!

學學老外這麼說

A：What a nice, even tan! You've been to the beach?

B：I just got back from Nice.

A：你的皮膚晒得好漂亮！你去了海灘？

B：我剛從尼斯回來。

單字

tan [tæn] n.
晒黑的膚色

---

* suntan [`sʌnˌtæn] n. 晒成褐色的膚色

102

我的皮膚因為晒傷而紅腫脫皮。

這句可以這麼說

I am **sunburnt** and my skin is all red, **swollen**, and **peeling**.

I have a sunburn, so my skin is red, swollen, and **flaky**.

學學老外這麼說

A : I am sunburnt, and my skin is all red, swollen, and peeling.

B : Cool water and *aloe gel may soothe your skin and relieve some pain.

A : 我被晒傷了，全身紅腫脫皮。

B : 涼水和蘆薈膠應該能幫你減輕一些痛苦。

---

* aloe gel 蘆薈凝膠。

單字

sunburnt
[`sʌn͵bɝnt] adj.
晒傷的

swollen [`swolən]
adj. 腫大的

peel [pil] v.
脫皮；外層脫落

flaky [`flekɪ] adj.
薄片的；呈裂開的
薄片的

我對很多品牌的保養品過敏。

這句可以這麼說

My skin is **allergic** to many skincare brands.

I am allergic to many skincare brands.

I have an allergy to many skincare brands.

學學老外這麼說

A：My skin is dry and sensitive. I have an allergy to many skincare brands.

B：I heard L´ORÈAL products do not **irritate** sensitive skin.

A：我的皮膚又乾又敏感。我對很多品牌的保養品過敏。

B：我聽說巴黎萊雅的產品不會刺激皮膚。

單字

allergic [əˋlɝˏdʒɪk]
adj. 敏感的；過敏的

irritate [ˋɪrəˏtet] v.
刺激

104

我快被臉上的青春痘煩死了。

這句可以這麼說

My **acne** really **sucks**.

My acne is so frustrating.

My acne on my face is so annoying.

I am fed up with my ***acne-prone** skin.

學學老外這麼說

A : My acne really sucks.

B : Try Neutrogena Deep Clean cleanser.

A : 我快被臉上的青春痘煩死了。

B : 試試露得清的深層清潔洗面乳。

單字

acne [ˋæknɪ] n. 青春痘；痤瘡

suck [sʌk] v. （俚）（對事情）感到厭煩；作嘔

---

* acne-prone 容易長青春痘的。

T 字部位老是出油、長粉刺怎麼辦？

這句可以這麼說

What can I do about my oily and **pimply** T-zone?

How can I cure my oily and pimply T-zone?

How can I make my oily T-zone clear and **spotless**?

Do you have any skincare advice for my oily and pimply T-zone?

學學老外這麼說

A : My T-zone is an absolute mess. How can I make it clear and spotless?

B : Use Proactiv Solution Refining Mask 3 times a week. You'll be amazed by the results.

A : 我的 T 字部位糟透了。怎麼才能去油不長青春痘？

B : 每週用三次高倫雅芙去痘緊緻面膜。結果會讓你吃驚的。

單字

pimply [`pɪmplɪ]
adj. 長滿粉刺的

spotless [`spɑtləs]
adj. 沒有汙點的；無瑕疵的

MP3
075

怎麼清除鼻頭上的黑頭粉刺？

這句可以這麼說

How should I remove the **blackheads** on my nose?

How can I ***get rid of** the blackheads on my nose?

How can I cure my ***strawberry nose**?

What's the best way to ***eliminate** the blackheads on my nose?

學學老外這麼說

A : What's the best way to eliminate the blackheads on my nose?

B : Buy a blackhead remover. The Biore pore strips are good.

A : 清除鼻子上的黑頭粉刺要用什麼方法最好？

B : 去買黑頭粉刺產品啊！蜜妮的妙鼻貼不錯。

---

* get rid of something / somebody 擺脫某事 / 某人。

* strawberry nose 草莓鼻；多指毛孔粗大、長滿黑頭粉刺以及發紅的鼻子。

* eliminate [ɪ`lɪmə‚net] v. 清除；消滅（敵人）。

單字

blackhead
[`blæk‚hɛd] n.
黑頭粉刺

除痘有方

Rinse your face with warm water and mild soap. Don't scrub too hard and overclean. （洗臉要用溫水，中性肥皂。不要用力擦洗和過度清洗。）

Avoid using too much makeup and wearing it to bed. （別用太多化妝品，避免沒卸妝就上床睡覺。）

Change your pillowcase often. （勤換枕頭套。）

Dump some myths about what eliminates the acne, such as sunbathing. （不要亂用偏門的除痘方法，例如：日晒除痘。）

Live a healthy life: Eat and drink healthily, reduce stress, and exercise. （生活方式要健康：飲食健康、減少壓力和多運動。）

Try some home remedies: apples, bananas, papaya, pineapple, strawberries, peach, and lemon as ingredients, etc. （自製小配方：用蘋果、香蕉、青木瓜、鳳梨、草莓、桃子、檸檬等原料。）

MP3
076

我的嘴唇一到冬天就乾裂。

這句可以這麼說

My lips **chap** in winter.

I have dry and chapped lips in winter.

My lips are dry and cracked in winter.

學學老外這麼說

A : My lips are dry and chapped in winter, and they even peel sometimes.

B : You can apply unflavored *lip balm to your lips to *alleviate these symptoms.

A：我的嘴唇一到冬天就乾裂，還會脫皮。

B：你可以抹一點沒有香味的護唇膏，能減緩症狀。

---

* balm [bɑm] n. 鎮痛軟膏；護膚膏。lip balm 則指「護唇膏」。

* alleviate [əˋlivɪˏet] v. 減輕；緩和。

單字

chap [tʃæp] v.
皮膚皸裂；乾裂

MP3
077

她的鼻子和兩頰全是雀斑。

這句可以這麼說

She has ***freckles** all over her nose and cheeks.
There are freckles all over her nose and cheeks.

學學老外這麼說

A : Look at that ugly girl. She has freckles all over her
nose and cheeks.
B : I think she is pretty.

A : 那個女孩真醜，她的鼻子和兩頰都是雀斑！
B : 我覺得她挺漂亮的。

---

* freckle [ˋfrɛkl] n. 指「雀斑；斑點」，常用複數形。

小笑話一則

Freckles and Wrinkles

An elderly woman and her little grandson, whose face was sprinkled with bright freckles, spent the day at the zoo. Lots of children were waiting in line to get their cheeks painted by a local artist, who was decorating them with tiger paws. "You've got so many freckles, there's no place to paint!" a girl in the line said to the little boy.

Embarrassed, the little boy dropped his head. His grandmother knelt down next to him. "I love your freckles. When I was a little girl, I always wanted freckles," she said, while tracing her finger across the child's cheek. "Freckles are beautiful."

The boy looked up, "Really?"

"Of course," said the grandmother. "Why, just name me one thing that's prettier than freckles."

The little boy thought for a moment, peered intensely into his grandma's face, and softly whispered, "Wrinkles."

雀斑和皺紋

一個老太太和她滿臉雀斑的小孫子一起去逛動物園。很多小孩正排隊等著讓當地的一個畫家在他們臉上畫老虎腳印。「你臉上這麼多雀斑，已經沒有地方畫啦！」隊伍中的一個小女孩對這個小男孩說。

小男孩尷尬地垂下了腦袋。他的奶奶蹲下來對他說：「我很喜歡你的雀斑。我還小的時候一直想要有雀斑。」她邊說，邊用手指撫摸他的臉。「雀斑很漂亮。」

小男孩抬起頭，「真的嗎？」

「當然，」奶奶說：「哦，不然你告訴我一樣比雀斑更漂亮的東西。」

小男孩思考了一會，非常仔細地看著奶奶的臉，然後輕輕地低聲說道：「皺紋。」

隨著年齡增長，我的臉上出現黃褐斑。

這句可以這麼說

As I got older, **chloasma** showed up on my face.

Dark **patches** developed on my face through the years.

學學老外這麼說

A：As I got older, chloasma showed up on my face.

B：It's partly due to your pregnancy. Use some **sunscreen** when you are outdoors.

A：隨著年齡增長，我的臉上出現黃褐斑。

B：部分是你懷孕的緣故。出門時抹點防晒油。

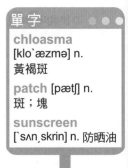

單字

chloasma
[klo`æzmə] n.
黃褐斑

patch [pætʃ] n.
斑；塊

sunscreen
[`sʌn‚skrin] n. 防晒油

好羨慕你紅潤又有光澤的膚色！

這句可以這麼說

How I envy your beautiful, ***glowing** ***skin tone**!

I really envy your gorgeous glowing skin!

Your skin has a real childlike glow! How I envy you!

I can't help being jealous of your gorgeous, ***radiant** skin!

學學老外這麼說

A : I really envy your gorgeous glowing skin.

B : To be frank, I prefer your ***porcelain-like** skin.

A : 真羨慕你紅潤又有光澤的皮膚。

B : 說實話，我更喜歡你像白瓷娃娃般的肌膚。

---

* glowing 指「容光煥發的」。注意，不能用 shiny 形容皮膚有光澤；因為
  shiny 用在形容皮膚時是指因油光而發亮。

* skin tone 膚色。

* radiant [`redɪənt] adj. 容光煥發的。

* porcelain-like 白瓷一般的。

單字

glowing [`gloɪŋ]
adj. 容光煥發的

113

MP3
080

你的臉色看起來暗沉。

Your skin looks **dull**.

You look a bit **sallow**.

Your skin has lost its tone.

學學老外這麼說

A : What has happened to you lately? Your skin looks dull.

B : I have been staying up late to finish my report.

A : 你最近怎麼了？你的臉色看起來很暗沉。

B : 我一直在熬夜寫報告。

單字

dull [dʌl] n.
暗沉的

sallow [`sælo] n.
皮膚或臉色發黃

Celery

After my husband asked me to help him shed some unwanted pounds, I stopped serving fattening TV snacks and substituted crisp celery.

While he was unenthusiastically munching on a stalk one night, a commercial caught his attention. As he watched longingly, a woman spread gooey chocolate frosting over a freshly baked cake.

When it was over, my husband turned to me. "Did you ever notice," he asked, "that they never advertise celery on TV?"

芹菜

從我老公要我幫他減重開始，我就不讓他在看電視時吃會長贅肉的零食，改要他吃脆脆的芹菜棒。

一天晚上當他毫無興致地嚼著一根芹菜棒時，一個電視廣告吸引了他。他憧憬地看著廣告裡的一個女生，把剛烤好的蛋糕抹上濃濃的巧克力漿。

廣告結束後，我老公轉過頭對我說。「你有沒有注意到，」他說：「他們從來不在電視上做芹菜廣告。」

抬頭紋、皺眉紋和笑紋一直困擾我。

這句可以這麼說

I'm depressed about the wrinkles on my forehead, my frown lines, and my laugh lines.

My forehead wrinkles, frown lines, and laugh lines are really annoying.

I am so upset with the wrinkles on my forehead, my frown lines and laugh lines.

My forehead wrinkles, frown lines and laugh lines are bothering me.

學學老外這麼說

A：My forehead wrinkles, frown lines, and laugh lines are really annoying

B：Have you tried the *anti-wrinkle and *anti-aging products by Estee Lauder?

A：抬頭紋、皺眉紋和笑紋一直困擾我。

B：你有沒有試過雅詩蘭黛的抗皺抗衰老產品？

---

* anti-wrinkle 抗皺。

* anti-aging 抗老。

MP3
082

我的眼角有很深的魚尾紋。

這句可以這麼說

I'm getting deep *crow's feet.

Deep crow's feet are developing around my eyes.

Deep crow's feet are showing up around my eyes.

學學老外這麼說

A : Deep crow's feet are showing up around my eyes. I have **saggy** skin already!

B : Don't talk like that. You are still young.

A : 我的眼角有很深的魚尾紋，我的皮膚已經鬆垮了！

B : 別這樣說，你還年輕呢！

單字
saggy [ˋsægɪ] adj.
鬆弛的；下陷的

---

* 中文用「魚尾」，英文則用「烏鴉的腳爪（crow's feet）」來形容眼尾的皺紋。

眼袋讓人看起來比較老。

這句可以這麼說

*Bags under your eyes betray your age.

Having bags under your eyes makes you look older.

Swollen, *puffy eyes make people look older.

學學老外這麼說

A : The bags under my eyes betray my age. I look terrible today. What can I do?

B : Put two iron spoons in the refrigerator for about ten minutes. Then press the spoons onto the bags.

A : 眼袋讓人看起來比較老。我今天看起來很糟糕，怎麼辦？

B : 放兩隻湯匙到冰箱冰十分鐘，然後把它們輕輕按在眼袋上。

---

* bags under your eyes 眼袋；也稱 baggy eyes。

* puffy eyes 泡泡眼；眼袋。

如何保持肌膚年輕？(1)

Drink plenty of water to clear your skin. （多喝水使皮膚潔淨。）

Avoid junk food, instant food, and fast food. （避免垃圾食品、調理包和速食。）

Eat plenty of leafy vegetables and fruits. （多吃綠葉蔬菜和水果。）

Use sunscreen to protect your skin from direct sunlight. （塗抹防晒乳保護皮膚，避免陽光直晒。）

Don't smoke cigarettes or drink alcohol. （不要抽菸、喝酒。）

Too much stress is also bad for your skin and body. （壓力太大也會傷身傷皮膚。）

Exercise to improve your blood circulation. （運動可增加血液循環。）

Get enough sleep, six to eight hours a night, and avoid staying up past 1:00 a.m. （每天睡足六到八小時，避免凌晨一點後才睡覺。）

MP3
084

黑眼圈是很常見的皮膚問題。

這句可以這麼說

*Dark circles under the eyes are a common beauty problem.

Dark circles under the eyes are one common skin complaint.

Almost everyone has had dark circles under their eyes.

學學老外這麼說

A : Look at the dark circles under my eyes.

B : Don't worry. Almost everyone has had them. Just get some sleep.

A : 你看我的黑眼圈。

B : 別擔心，這幾乎每個人都會有的，好好睡個覺就行了。

---

* dark circle(s) 指「（因睡眠不足等而引起的）黑眼圈」，若因被揍、撞到硬物
  而引起的眼周淤青，要用 black eye。

120

黑眼圈和眼袋的持久戰

Get plenty of sleep nightly. （晚上睡眠要充足。）

Use overnight facial masks to treat your skin while you sleep. （睡覺時利用夜間面膜保養皮膚。）

Apply cool tea bags, an ice cube wrapped in a soft cloth, or cucumber slices to your eyes daily. （每天使用冰涼的茶包、冰塊用軟布包好來敷眼睛，用小黃瓜片也行。）

Apply an eye cream containing vitamin K and retinol. （塗抹含維生素 K 和維生素 A 的眼霜。）

Avoid rubbing your eyes. （避免揉眼睛。）

Eat a healthy, balanced diet, take vitamins, and drink plenty of water. （飲食要健康、均衡、吃點維他命以及大量喝水。）

Reduce salt intake. （減少鹽分攝取。）

Snack on bananas and raisins. （把香蕉和葡萄乾當零食。）

Drink cabbage or cranberry juice. （喝一些高麗菜或蔓越莓汁。）

Quit smoking. （戒菸。）

02 保養品

MP3
085

這系列的保養品適合哪個年齡層？

這句可以這麼說

Which age group is this set of skincare products for?

What age group would need this set of skincare products?

What is the target age group for this set of skincare products?

學學老外這麼說

A : Which age group is this set of skincare products for? Are these skincare products for women under 25?

B : No. They are for women from 30 to 45.

A : 這系列的保養品適合哪個年齡層？這些保養品適合二十五歲以下的女性嗎？

B : 不太適合。這產品針對的是三十到四十五歲的女性。

MP3
086

乾性膚質要用什麼洗面乳啊？

這句可以這麼說

What *facial cleansers are good for dry skin?

What face wash would you recommend for a dry skin?

學學老外這麼說

A : What facial cleansers are good for dry skin?

B : I recommend the Burt's Bees Wild Lettuce
 Complexion Soap.

A : 乾性膚質要用什麼洗面乳啊？

B : 我推薦蜜蜂爺爺野萵苣潤膚皂。

單字
complexion
[kəm`plɛkʃən] n.
面色；臉色；容貌

* facial cleanser / face wash 洗面乳。

我喜歡用泡沫洗面乳。

這句可以這麼說

I prefer a face wash *foam.

I like a *foaming face wash better.

學學老外這麼說

A : This Olay **Aqua** Hydration Cleansing Milk doesn't foam. I prefer a foaming face wash.

B : But experts say that foaming cleansers are not necessarily more effective than milky ones.

A : 歐蕾水潤洗面乳沒有泡沫。我還是喜歡泡沫洗面乳。

B : 但專家說泡沫的不一定比乳液洗面乳有效。

單字

aqua [ˋækwə] n. 水；溶液

---

* foam [fom] n. 泡沫 v. 起泡沫。face wash foam / foaming face wash 泡沫洗面乳。

MP3
088

潔顏磨砂膏有去角質的效果。

這句可以這麼說

A facial **scrub** removes dead skin cells.

A facial scrub ***exfoliates** dead skin cells.

學學老外這麼說

A : You can use this facial scrub twice a week to exfoliate dead skin cells.

B : Is there also a body scrub?

A : Yes. Here it is.

A : 你可以每週用兩次潔顏磨砂膏來清除老化角質。

B : 是不是還有身體磨砂膏？

A : 有的，在這裡。

---

* exfoliate 在美容中指「去角質」。

單字

scrub [skrʌb] n.
擦洗；這裡指的是
有去角質功效的磨
砂膏

exfoliate
[ɛks`folɪ.et] n.
使（皮膚，樹皮
等）片狀剝落

洗臉大作戰

用溫水洗臉，用手輕搓，還要選適合的潔顏乳，而不是選貴的。

潔顏乳有什麼種類？

face wash foam 潔顏泡沫

face wash milk 潔顏乳

face wash cream 潔顏霜

face wash gel 潔顏凝膠

facial scrub 潔顏磨砂膏，有沙沙的觸感。

根據不同的膚質和肌膚問題，又有不同種類：

Gentle foaming facial cleanser for normal skin 中性肌膚專用的溫和泡沫潔顏乳

White radiance facial cleanser for dull skin 暗沉肌膚專用的美白潔顏乳

Hydra-Cleansing facial cleanser for dry skin 乾性肌膚專用的水潤潔顏乳

Revitalizing facial cleanser for mature skin 老化肌膚專用的煥膚潔顏乳

Aloe calming facial cleanser for sensitive skin 敏感肌膚專用的蘆薈鎮靜潔顏乳

Oil-free acne face wash for oily and pimply skin 油性及青春痘肌膚專用的清爽除痘潔顏乳

我想看看化妝水。

Could I see some skin **toners**?

Can I see your selection of toners?

Can you show me the toners, please?

I'd like to try some toners, please.

A : I'd like to try some toners, please.

B : Here are the testers.

A : 我想看看化妝水。

B : 這些是試用品。

單字

toner [`tonɚ] n.
化妝水

需要每天用化妝水嗎？

這句可以這麼說

Is it necessary to use a facial toner in my daily skin care?

Do I need to use a facial toner in my daily skin care?

Is a facial toner necessary in my daily skin care?

學學老外這麼說

A : Is it necessary to use a facial toner in my daily skin care?

B : No, unless you have really oily skin. For dry skin, alcohol-free *smoothing toners** are preferable.

A : 需要每天用化妝水嗎？

B : 不需要，除非你的皮膚很會出油。乾性皮膚最好用不含酒精的柔膚水。

---

* smoothing toner 柔膚水。

這款柔膚水很保溼。

這句可以這麼說

The smoothing toner has very good moisturizing effects.

My skin feels moist all day after using this smoothing toner.

I love this moisturizing ***facial mist**.

This ***facial spray** is a really good moisturizer.

學學老外這麼說

A : The smoothing toner has very good moisturizing effects.

B : I'll give it a try.

A : 這款柔膚水很保溼。

B : 我會試試看。

---

* facial mist / facial spray 保溼噴霧，也可以當柔膚水用。

MP3
092

玫瑰水能舒緩和收斂敏感肌膚。

這句可以這麼說

Rose water can **soothe** and **refine** your sensitive skin.

Rose water has very good soothing and refining effects on sensitive skin.

學學老外這麼說

A : After using rose water, I noticed I had brighter skin, a more even skin tone, and hardly any **blemishes**.

B : Yes, it has very good soothing and refining effects on sensitive skin.

A : 用過玫瑰水後，我覺得皮膚變透亮，膚色更均勻，幾乎沒長斑了。

B : 對，它可以舒緩和收斂敏感肌膚。

單字

soothe [suð] v.
鎮靜；舒緩

refine [rɪ`faɪn] v.
收斂；緊緻

blemish [`blɛmɪʃ]
n. 斑點；痕跡

解開化妝水之謎

化妝水是不是護膚必須品？一些專家認為不是。但多數人都說：「化妝水讓我的皮膚保持乾淨及清新。」（A facial toner can keep my skin clean and fresh.）實際上，很多化妝水都含酒精、水楊酸、乙醇酸和羥基酸（alcohol, salicylic acid, glycolic acid, and hydroxyl acid），是專為油性和青春痘肌膚設計的。其實針對不同膚質，化妝水也有無酒精保溼潤澤化妝水（alcohol-free moisturizing toner），細緻毛孔收斂水（pore refining toner），純淨喚膚水（clarifying and revitalizing toner）等。

一般細分為：

toner / tonic / astringent 化妝水（適合中性膚質）

firming lotion 收斂水（適合油性長青春痘膚質）

smoothing toner 柔膚水（適合乾性膚質）

這裡特別提一下，集萬千寵愛於一身的玫瑰水（rose water），皮膚敏感的年輕女孩不要錯過喲！

這種潤膚露效果不錯。

這句可以這麼說

This **moisturizer** is really good.

This moisturizer really helps my skin retain moisture.

This moisturizer really keeps skin hydrated.

This moisturizer can really prevent dryness.

學學老外這麼說

A : This moisturizer really keeps skin hydrated.

B : Really? It's cool.

A : 這種潤膚露真的很保溼吧！

B : 真的啊？那滿讚的。

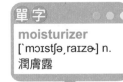

單字
moisturizer
[`mɔɪstʃə͵raɪzə] n.
潤膚露

日霜和晚霜能混用嗎？

HOPE PLANET

這句可以這麼說

Can a *day cream and a *night cream be used interchangeably?

Can a night cream be used during the daytime, and *vice versa?

Are there big differences between a day cream and a night cream?

學學老外這麼說

A：Are there big differences between a day cream and a night cream?

B：A day cream has less oil and moisturizes your skin, while a night cream repairs your skin.

A：日霜和晚霜有什麼差別嗎？

B：日霜含油分少，主要的作用是肌膚保溼，而晚霜則是肌膚修復。

---

* day cream 日霜；night cream 晚霜。

* vice versa 反之亦然。

單字
cream [krim] n.
乳霜

你用過這種海藻泥面膜嗎？

> **這句可以這麼說**

Have you tried this seaweed mud *facial mask?

Have you used a seaweed mud facial mask before?

Do you know about this seaweed mud facial mask?

> **學學老外這麼說**

A : Have you used a seaweed mud facial mask before?
It's very popular.

B : No. It's for oily skin. I use a hydrating or radiance
facial mask. Sometimes firming masks.

A : How about this *peel-off facial mask?

B : I prefer a rinse-off mask.

A : 你用過海藻泥面膜嗎？它很受歡迎。

B : 沒有，它適合油性膚質。我通常用保溼或者修護面膜，有時候用緊
緻面膜。

A : 那這種撕除式面膜呢？

B : 我比較喜歡可沖洗的面膜。

---

* facial mask 面膜。

* peel [pil] v. 去皮。peel-off 撕除。

沐浴乳比香皂更保溼嗎？

這句可以這麼說

Does ***body wash** have a better moisturizing effect than ***toilet soap**?

Does body wash or toilet soap retain more moisture?

Does body wash have better hydration effects than toilet soap?

學學老外這麼說

A：Does body wash or toilet soap retain more moisture? Soaps dry out my skin.

B：Do they? In fact, new soaps or bath soaps can also keep your skin moist.

A：沐浴乳比香皂更保溼嗎？香皂會讓我的皮膚乾乾的。

B：是嗎？事實上，有些新款香皂或沐浴皂也能鎖水保溼。

---

* body wash 沐浴乳。

* toilet soap 香皂。

135

老牌子凡士林的身體乳液還是很好用。

▶ 這句可以這麼說

The old brand Vaseline body lotion still works well.

The body lotion by the old brand Vaseline still has very good moisturizing effects.

The old brand Vaseline is still popular after all these years.

▶ 學學老外這麼說

A : Can you recommend a good body lotion?

B : The old brand Vaseline body lotion still works well.

A：能為我推薦好用的身體乳液嗎？

B：老牌子凡士林的身體乳液還是很好用。

保養品的語言

balancing 平衡的

clarifying 清新的

deep cleaning 深層清潔的

exfoliating 去角質的

firming 緊緻的

hydrating 保溼的

nourishing 滋養的

purifying 純淨的

radiating 亮膚的

refreshing 醒膚的

rejuvenating 回春駐顏的

revitalizing 活膚煥膚的

whitening 美白的

如何保持肌膚年輕？(2)

Use a cotton pad soaked with apple cider vinegar to clean your dry skin. （用化妝棉沾蘋果醋清潔乾燥皮膚。）

Apply organic olive oil to moisturize your skin before going to bed. （睡前可以塗抹有機橄欖油來滋潤皮膚。）

Wash your skin with a chemical free skin cleanser or lotion. （用不含化學物質的洗面乳或潔顏水。）

Meditation and yoga are good ways to relax. （靜坐和瑜伽能讓你放鬆。）

這種美白產品含汞和類固醇。

This whitening product contains **mercury** and **steroids**.

This whitening product tested positive for mercury and steroids.

Mercury and steroids were found in this whitening product.

A：It is reported that this whitening product contains mercury and steroids. They may cause mental problems and skin problems.

B：Thank God that I've never used it.

A：報導說這種美白產品含汞和類固醇，可能導致精神和皮膚問題。

B：謝天謝地，還好我從沒用過。

單字

mercury [ˋmɝkjərɪ] n. 汞

steroid [ˋstɪrɔɪd] n. 類固醇

MP3 099

這種日霜的防晒係數是十五。

這句可以這麼說

This day cream has an ***SPF** of 15.

The SPF of this day cream is 15.

This is an SPF 15 day cream.

學學老外這麼說

A：Does this day cream have an SPF number?

B：Yes, it has an SPF of 15. Good enough for summer mornings and evenings.

A：這款日霜防晒嗎？

B：可以，它的防晒係數是十五。夏天早晚用都夠。

---

* SPF = sun protection factor 防晒係數。

這種防晒乳能防紫外線（UV）嗎？

Does this sunscreen offer protection against *UV?
Can this sunscreen block out UV light effectively?
Does this sunscreen block UV light?

A : Does this sunscreen offer protection against *UVA?
B : Yes. This sign, PA++, means 8 hours of protection.
A : 這種防晒乳能防紫外線嗎？
B : 可以。這個 PA++ 標誌表示能防紫外線八小時。

* UV 紫外（線）的。UVA 紫外線。

這種防晒乳防水嗎？

這句可以這麼說

Is this sunblock **waterproof**?

Is this sunblock ***sweat-proof**?

Can I wear this sunblock while swimming?

學學老外這麼說

A : Is this sunblock waterproof?

B : Yes, you can sweat and swim without worrying
    about it.

A : 這種防晒乳防水嗎？

B : 沒問題。流汗和游泳都不用擔心。

單字

waterproof
[`wotɚ͵pruf] n. 防水

* sweat-proof 防汗。

美白大戰：防晒

美容天王大 S 美白防晒達到鐵面人和助理撐傘如影相隨的地步，可見防晒的重要性。防晒有哪些小陷阱呢？

suntan lotion 和 sunscreen 的區別：亞洲年輕女孩都愛白皙肌膚，而歐美近來推崇 suntan girl。suntan 防晒傷，但追求晒黑，亞洲女孩如果買錯產品，可就後悔莫及了。

sunscreen 和 sunblock 的差別：中文一樣，東西還是有很大不同。sunblock 塗在身上美白，防晒效果好。而 sunscreen 塗抹後不明顯，且幾小時後，就要補充一次。

day cream 和 night cream 的區別：日霜有防晒作用（A day cream has an SPF number.）。不過，你了解白天防晒如果用晚霜，可能會出現什麼後果呢？答案是晒傷。因為有些晚霜可能含有維生素 A（Retinol），是光敏感物質，容易引起陽光過敏。

UVB 和 UVA 的區別：如果你買的防晒乳只有 SPF 而沒有 PA+，那麼它只能防 UVB。UVB 主要會導致晒傷（sunburn），而 UVA 除了晒傷還會晒黑（suntan）。

薰衣草精油能安神和舒緩皮膚。

這句可以這麼說

Lavender *essential oil** soothes your skin and nerves.

Lavender essential oil has a good soothing effect on your skin and nerves.

Lavender essential oil can be used to relax your skin and nerves.

學學老外這麼說

A : I had another sleepless night. I look older.

B : Use some lavender essential oil in your bath. It has a good soothing effect on your skin and nerves.

A : 我昨晚又睡不著。我看起來更老了。

B : 泡澡的時候用點薰衣草精油，對皮膚和精神的舒緩效果很好。

單字
lavender
[ˈlævəndɚ] n.
薰衣草

* essential [ɪˈsɛnʃəl] adj. 基本的，根本的。essential oil 精油。

眼膠較清爽，不容易長肉芽。

***Eye gels** are light and usually treat **milia**.

Light eye gels don't cause milia around the eyes.

With a light eye gel, you won't develop ***milia seeds** around your eyes.

A : Look at the dark circles under your eyes. You need an eye cream.

B : But eye creams may leave milia around my eyes.

A : Eye gels are light and usually treat milia.

A : 看看你的黑眼圈！你得用眼霜了！

B : 但是用眼霜會讓我長肉芽。

A : 眼膠較清爽，不容易長肉芽。

單字

milia [ˋmɪlɪəm] n.
（醫）粟丘疹

---

* eye gel 護眼凝膠。

* milia seeds 指「（皮膚上的）脂肪粒」。

MP3
104

我每週用兩次眼膜。

I use *eye masks** twice a week.

I apply eye masks to my eyes twice a week.

I have eye mask treatments twice a week.

A : How do you make your eyes look so young?

B : I have eye mask treatments twice a week. They're very convenient and moisturizing.

A : 你怎麼保養你的眼睛，可以看起來這麼年輕？

B : 我每週用兩次眼膜。它很方便也很保溼。

---

* eye mask 眼膜。

你可以試試這款活膚乳液。

這句可以這麼說

Try this ***facial lift emulsion**.

Give this facial lift emulsion a try.

學學老外這麼說

A : Why don't you give this facial lift emulsion a try?
    It's quite good.

B : OK.

A : 要不要試看看這款活膚乳液？很讚喔。

B : 好哇。

---

* facial lift emulsion 活膚乳液。

Cosmetics

Luke's wife bought a new line of expensive cosmetics guaranteed to make her look years younger. After sitting for a long time in front of the mirror applying the "miracle" products she asked, "Darling, honestly, what age would you say I am?"
Looking over her carefully, Luke replied, "Judging from your skin, twenty; your hair, eighteen; and your figure, twenty-five."
"Oh, you flatterer!" she gushed.
"Hey, wait a minute!" Luke interrupted. "I haven't added them up yet."

化妝品

路克的妻子買了一系列昂貴的化妝品，據說保證能讓她看起來年輕好幾歲。坐在鏡子前抹這種「奇蹟」化妝品很長一段時間後，她問道：「親愛的，老實告訴我，現在我看起來像幾歲？」
路克很仔細地看過她之後，回答：「從你的皮膚看，20；頭髮，18；身材，25。」
「你真會讚美人！」她感動地說。
「喂，等一下！」路克打斷妻子，「我還沒有把這些數字加起來呢！」

MP3
106

我的眉毛又稀又淡。

這句可以這麼說

My **eyebrows** are thin and light.

I have very thin and light eyebrows.

How I wish I had your thick eyebrows!

學學老外這麼說

A : My eyebrows are thin and light.

B : I can add some ***definition** and color to your eyebrows.

A : 我的眉毛又稀又淡。

B : 我可以讓你的眉毛輪廓顏色都鮮明點。

單字
eyebrow [ˋaɪ.brau] n. 眉毛

---

* definition [.dɛfəˋnɪʃən] n. 清晰度；（輪廓）清晰。

你的眉毛修得很漂亮。

這句可以這麼說

Your eyebrows are beautifully **groomed**.

You have beautifully groomed and shaped eyebrows.

You really know how to groom your eyebrows.

學學老外這麼說

A：Your eyebrows are beautifully groomed and shaped.

B：Thank you.

A：你的眉毛修得真漂亮。

B：謝謝。

單字

groom [grum] v.
打扮；修飾

MP3
108

粗眉毛看起來更自然。

這句可以這麼說

Thick eyebrows give you a more natural look.
Thick eyebrows look more natural.

學學老外這麼說

A : Keep ***plucking** and **tweezing** to a minimum.
B : Why?
A : Thick eyebrows look more natural.

A : 眉毛盡量少拔一些。

B : 為什麼啊？

A : 粗眉毛看起來更自然。

單字
tweeze [twiz] v.
用鑷子拔除

---

* pluck [plʌk] v. 拔去（眉毛）。

MP3
109

你的貓眼妝讓眼睛很出色。

The *cat's eye look highlights your eyes.

The cat's eye look enhances your eyes.

The cat's eye look adds drama to your eyes.

The cat's eye look really emphasizes your eyes.

學學老外這麼說

A : The cat's eye look really adds drama to your eyes.

B : Thank you. Your smoky eyes are very stylish, too.

A：你的貓眼妝讓眼睛很出色。

B：謝謝。你的煙燻眼妝也很時尚。

---

* cat's eye look 貓眼妝。

MP3
110

戴假睫毛不舒服。

這句可以這麼說

***False eyelashes** irritate my eyelids.

False eyelashes make me **itch** a lot.

False eyelashes are uncomfortable to wear.

學學老外這麼說

A : I don't like to wear false eyelashes. They're uncomfortable to wear.

B : Me neither. Good **mascara** does an even better job.

A：我不喜歡戴假睫毛，戴起來感覺不舒服。

B：我也不喜歡。好的睫毛膏比較好用。

單字

itch [ɪtʃ] v. 癢

mascara
[mæs`kærə] n.
睫毛膏

---

* false eyelash(es) 假睫毛。

怎樣讓睫毛又長又密？

這句可以這麼說

How can I get long thick eyelashes?

How can I create long thick eyelashes?

Do you have tips for making long thick eyelashes?

Can you recommend a good mascara for long thick eyelashes?

學學老外這麼說

A : How did you get such long thick eyelashes?

B : I curl my lashes with an ***eyelash curler** first. Then I apply a tiny bit of Vaseline. And last, cover them with a layer of Maybelline mascara.

A : 你怎麼讓睫毛又長又密？

B : 我先把睫毛夾翹，然後塗一點凡士林，最後再塗一層媚比琳的睫毛膏。

---

* eyelash curler 睫毛夾。

To enlarge small eyes 小眼變大眼

Apply a medium-toned shadow （such as soft grey or blue） to the crease. （在眼褶上塗中間色調的眼影〔如柔和灰色或藍色〕。）

Use a soft-coloured liner （try taupe） on the top and bottom lash lines. （用柔和顏色的眼線筆畫上下眼線〔試試灰棕色〕。）

Apply black mascara on the upper lashes. （在上眼睫毛上塗黑色睫毛膏。）

Apply a light shadow on the eyelids. （眼瞼上塗淺色眼影。）

Apply more intense shades in the creases. （在眼褶上加重顏色。）

Add lift to the outer corners. （外眼角上描。）

亞洲女孩要注意，上面畫的是歐美系的眼妝，眼線到眼瞼為淺色眼影，往上到眼褶是深色眼影，適合眼窩較深的眼睛。如果眼窩不夠深，那麼第一步、第四步和第五步中提到的眼影顏色要換一下，也就是眼線到眼瞼眼瞼用深色眼影，往上到眼褶是淺色眼影。

你的粉底不均勻。

Your **foundation** is uneven.

Your foundation is **clumpy**.

You didn't apply your foundation evenly.

You need to **blend** the foundation well into your skin.

A : Is my foundation even?

B : No. Use a foundation brush, a sponge, or just your fingertips to spread it evenly.

A : 我的粉底均勻嗎？

B : 沒有。用粉底刷、海綿或者就用你的手指尖把它抹勻。

單字

foundation
[faun`deʃən] n. 粉底

clumpy [`klʌmpɪ]
adj. 結塊的

blend [blɛnd] v.
調和；打勻

155

腮紅能讓蒼白的臉看起來有活力。

這句可以這麼說

Some blush will brighten up your *pale skin.

Apply some *blush to add color to your face.

You need some blush to cheer up your face.

學學老外這麼說

A : You look pale today. What you need is some blush to cheer up your face.

B : Yeah. It may cheer me up.

A : 你今天看起來很蒼白,你需要腮紅讓臉色看起來有活力。

B : 對。或許也能讓我心情好點。

單字

pale [pel] adj.
蒼白的

---

* pale 亦可指天生白而無血色的;或病態狀的慘白膚色。

* blush / cheek color 腮紅。

MP3 114

我剛修了指甲，還塗了深紫色指甲油。

這句可以這麼說

I just had a **manicure** and applied deep purple[*] **fingernail polish**.

I just had a manicure and had my nails painted deep purple.

學學老外這麼說

A : Wow, deep purple fingernails.

B : Yeah, aren't they cool? I just had a manicure and applied deep purple fingernail polish.

A：哇，深紫色指甲！

B：對啊，酷吧？我剛修了指甲，還塗了深紫色指甲油。

單字
manicure
[ˋmænɪ.kjur] v. & n.
修剪指甲；美甲

---

* fingernail polish 指甲油。

她的妝太誇張了。

這句可以這麼說

Her makeup is too bold.

Her makeup is too dramatic.

Her makeup is really scary.

Her makeup is out of place.

She wears too much makeup.

She has tons of makeup on her face.

學學老外這麼說

A : She looks like a *drag queen with that heavy
makeup. It's too much.

B : She really shouldn't walk around in broad daylight.

A : 她看起來像是濃妝豔抹的扮裝皇后，太誇張了。

B : 她確實不該在大白天就這樣跑到大街上來。

---

* drag queen 男扮女裝者。

MP3
116

她的裸妝恰到好處。

Her *nude look is perfect.

She's wearing her makeup so *subtly and naturally.

She has a natural glow on her face, without looking made up.

A : How did you get that natural glow on your face, without looking made up?

B : It's called the nude look.

A : 你怎麼化的妝？看起來自然有光彩，又像沒化一樣。

B : 這叫裸妝。

---

* nude look 裸妝。

* subtly [`sʌtlɪ] adj. 巧妙的，敏銳的。

日妝不化深色眼影。

這句可以這麼說

Do not wear heavy ***eye shadow** in daytime.

Heavy eye shadow doesn't work well as ***daytime make-up**.

學學老外這麼說

A : I am going to a wedding in the daytime. Should I wear eye shadow?

B : Do not wear heavy eye shadow in daytime. A light eye shadow will do.

A : 我要在白天參加一個婚禮，要不要化眼影呢？

B : 日妝一般不化深色眼影，淡淡的眼影就可以了。

---

* eye shadow 眼影。

* day makeup 日妝。

MP3
118

你有沒有化晚妝的小技巧？

這句可以這麼說

Do you know any tricks for ***evening makeup**?

How can I apply makeup for an evening look?

What kind of makeup should I wear to a party?

學學老外這麼說

A : I am going to a party tonight. Do you know any tricks for evening makeup?

B : It has to be heavier than your day makeup. Use a darker eye shadow and eye liner. You may want to try the cat's eye look.

A : 我今晚要去一個舞會，有沒有什麼晚妝小技巧？

B : 晚妝要比日妝濃一些，用顏色深一點的眼影和眼線，你可以試試貓眼妝。

---

* evening makeup / party makeup 晚妝；晚宴妝。

MP3 119

你會化新娘妝嗎？

這句可以這麼說

Do you know any tricks for doing ***bridal makeup**?

Do you know how to apply bridal makeup?

What kind of makeup is good for a bride?

學學老外這麼說

A : Do you know how to apply bridal makeup? My sister wants to look sweet and innocent on her wedding day.

B : I suggest that she get intense skincare 2 weeks before the wedding first.

A : 你知道怎麼化新娘妝嗎？我妹妹想要在她的婚禮上看起來清純甜美。

B : 我建議她在婚禮前的兩個星期開始密集保養。

---

* bridal makeup 新娘妝。

Lipstick Prints

According to a radio report, a middle school in Oregon was faced with a unique problem. A number of girls were beginning to use lipstick and would put it on in the bathroom. That was fine, but after they put on their lipstick, they would press their lips to the mirrors, leaving dozens of little lip prints.

Finally, the principal decided that something had to be done. She called all the girls to the bathroom and met them there with the custodian. She explained that all these lip prints were causing a major problem for the custodian, who had to clean the mirrors every day.

To demonstrate how difficult it was to clean the mirrors, she asked the custodian to clean one of the mirrors. He proceeded to take out a long-handled brush, dip it into the nearest toilet, and scrub the mirror. Since then, there have been no lip prints on the mirrors.

口紅印

聽收音機報導說，奧勒崗州有所中學碰到一個很特別的問題。一些女孩開始塗口紅，而且是在洗手間裡。這沒有關係，問題是塗好口紅後，她們把嘴巴貼在鏡子上，留下許多口紅印。

最後，校長決定要採取行動。她要求所有的女學生到洗手間，然後她和管理員也一起到

現場。她解釋說，這些口紅印每天會給清潔鏡子的管理員帶來很大的困擾。為了示範清洗鏡子有多困難，她讓管理員清洗其中一面。管理員拿出一枝長柄刷，在最近的馬桶裡沾了水，開始擦鏡子。從此之後，鏡子上再也沒有出現口紅印了。

MP3
120

這個遮瑕膏蓋住了我的黑眼圈。

這句可以這麼說

This **concealer** covers the circles under my eyes well.

This concealer helps to hide the circles under my eyes.

This concealer is very effective in hiding the circles under my eyes.

This concealer works great with the circles under my eyes.

學學老外這麼說

A : The circles under my eyes are really annoying.

B : A concealer works great with them.

A : 我的黑眼圈很困擾我。

B : 遮瑕膏可以遮蓋住它們。

單 字

concealer
[`kʌnsilə] n. 遮瑕膏

你喜歡用粉底液還是粉餅？

這句可以這麼說

Do you like *liquid foundation or *pressed powder?

Do you prefer liquid foundation or pressed powder?

What type of foundation do you usually use? Liquid foundation or pressed powder?

學學老外這麼說

A：What type of foundation do you usually use?

B：I apply a liquid foundation first and then *loose powder.

A：你通常用什麼類型的粉底？

B：我會先用粉底液，然後再撲上一層蜜粉。

* liquid foundation 粉底液。
* pressed powder 粉餅。
* loose powder 蜜粉。

MP3
122

油性膚質用粉底霜比較好。

這句可以這麼說

A *__powder foundation__ works better for oily skin.

A powder foundation is good for oily skin.

學學老外這麼說

A : I have oily skin.

B : Then you'd better use a powder foundation.

A : 我是油性膚質。

B : 那你還是選粉底霜吧。

---

* powder foundation 粉底霜。

這款粉條有什麼顏色？

What colors do you have in this *stick foundation**?

How many colors does this stick foundation come in?

Has this stick foundation got other colors?

A：What colors do you have in this stick foundation?

B：White ivory, honey beige, sun glow, café au lait, and rose blush. The other colors are temporarily out of stock.

A：這款粉條有什麼顏色？

B：象牙白、蜂蜜褐、陽光金色、咖啡牛奶色還有玫瑰紅。其他顏色暫時缺貨。

---

* stick foundation 粉底棒；粉條。

MP3
124

淺色粉底適合我的膚色嗎?

這句可以這麼說

Will a light-colored foundation look good on my skin?

Should I choose a light-colored foundation?

Does a light **shade** suit my *****skin tone**?

Is a light shade right for my skin tone?

學學老外這麼說

A : Will a light-colored foundation look good on my skin?

B : I suggest a dark shade for your skin tone.

A : 淺色的粉底適合我的膚色嗎?

B : 我建議選適合你的深色粉底。

單字

shade [ʃed] n. 色調

---

* skin tone 膚色。

MP3
125

我的膚色該選什麼顏色的腮紅？

What blush should I choose for my skin tone?

How can I pick the right blush for my skin tone?

What blush flatters my pale tone?

Is this rosy blush good for my pale skin?

A : How can I pick the right blush for my skin tone?

B : Rosy or pink colors are better for fair skin. *Mauves
  or light *bronze are good for olive tones. And red or
  deep bronze for dark tones.

A : 我的膚色該選什麼顏色的腮紅？

B : 玫瑰色或粉色適合白皮膚；淡紫色或淡褐色適合橄欖色皮膚；紅色
  或深褐色適合深色皮膚。

---

* mauve [mov] n. 淡紫色。

* bronze [branz] n. 古銅色。

169

修容粉餅讓我的臉更有立體感。

這句可以這麼說

***Shading powder** adds **contours** to my face.

Shading powder corrects the shape of my face.

學學老外這麼說

A : How I wish I had an oval face.

B : You can apply some shading powder to add contours to your face.

A : 我好希望我有張瓜子臉！

B : 你可以用修容粉餅讓你的臉立體點。

單字

contour [ˋkɑntur]
n. 外形；輪廓

---

* shading powder 修容粉餅。

化妝包一覽

concealer 遮瑕膏

foundation 粉底

shading powder 修容粉餅

cheek color 腮紅

brow pencil 眉筆

brow powder 眉粉

eye liner 眼線筆

eye shadow 眼影

mascara 睫毛膏

lip liner 唇線筆

lipstick 唇膏

nail polish 指甲油

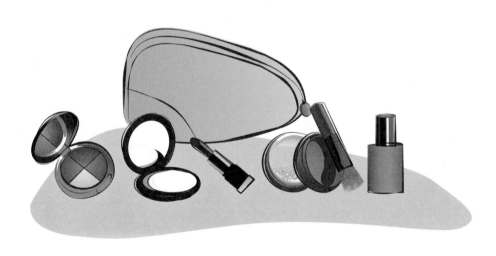

這款眉筆太軟容易斷。

這句可以這麼說

This *brow pencil is too soft.

This brow pencil is not hard enough.

This brow pencil breaks so easily.

學學老外這麼說

A : This brow pencil breaks so easily.

B : Use your fingertips when applying it. You can also try the Mac brow pencil.

A : 這款眉筆太軟容易斷了。

B : 用你的手指塗，也可以試試 **Mac** 的眉筆。

---

* brow pencil 眉筆。

什麼牌子的眉筆不容易掉色？

這句可以這麼說

What brow pencil doesn't come off easily?

What brow pencil doesn't fade easily?

What brow pencil has great staying power?

學學老外這麼說

A：What brow pencil has great staying power?

B：This L'Oréal Paris Brow Stylist Brow Liner is a good choice.

A：什麼牌子的眉筆不容易掉色？

B：這款巴黎萊雅的造型眉筆不錯。

眉粉適合細眉毛。

這句可以這麼說

*****Eyebrow powder** is just for thin brows.

Eyebrow powder is a good choice for a thin brows.

Eyebrow powder fills up thin brows perfectly.

Thin eyebrows can be better defined with eyebrow powder.

學學老外這麼說

A : Any tips for my thin eyebrows?

B : Eyebrow powder is just for thin brows. You can use an eyebrow pencil to fill them in and then apply eyebrow powder. It will look very natural.

A : 針對我的稀眉毛有什麼好的建議嗎？

B : 眉粉適合細眉毛。你可以先用眉筆填顏色，然後再撲上一點眉粉，這樣看起來會很自然。

---

* eyebrow powder 眉粉。

MP3
130

我用的是米白色眼影。

I am wearing beige eye shadow.

I am using a beige-colored eye shadow.

A : What eye shadow flatters brown eyes? I am wearing beige eye shadow now.

B : I suggest copper, bronze, champagne, beige and forest-green.

A : Well, I'll try champagne next time.

A : 什麼顏色眼影適合棕色眼睛？我現在是用米白色的眼影。

B : 我建議紅銅色、古銅色、香檳色、米白色和森林綠。

A : 那我下次來試香檳色。

這種睫毛膏有拉長的效果。

這句可以這麼說

This mascara makes your eyelashes look longer.

This is a lengthening mascara.

This mascara has extension effects.

學學老外這麼說

A : This mascara makes your eyelashes look longer.

B : Can I try it?

A : Sure.

A : 這種睫毛膏有拉長的效果。

B : 我能試試嗎？

A : 當然。

這款睫毛膏防水嗎？

這句可以這麼說

Is this mascara waterproof?

Is this a non-**smudging** mascara?

Can I wear this mascara in the heat of summer?

學學老外這麼說

A：Is this mascara waterproof?

B：Yes. Maybelline Lash Discovery is the best among waterproof mascaras.

A：這款睫毛膏防水嗎？

B：對。媚比琳驚豔亮眼睫毛膏是最好的防水型睫毛膏。

單字

smudge [smʌdʒ]
v. 弄模糊；弄髒

177

這款睫毛夾讓我的直睫毛變得又捲又翹。

這句可以這麼說

This eyelash curler makes my straight eyelashes really **curly**.

This eyelash curler works wonders on my straight eyelashes.

This eyelash curler is good for my straight eyelashes.

學學老外這麼說

A：This eyelash curler makes my straight eyelashes really curly.

B：Really? I'd like to try it.

A：這款睫毛夾讓我的直睫毛變得又捲又翹。

B：真的？我想試試看。

單字
curly [ˋkɝlɪ] adj.
捲翹的

MP3
134

這款唇膏買一送一。

This lipstick is *two-for-one.

Buy one lipstick of this kind, you can get another one free.

They're having a buy-one-get-one-free sale on this lipstick.

A : The Estee Lauder Signature Hydra *Luster Lipstick is on sale for two-for-one. I can buy a Rich Red one and get a Pink Champagne free.

B : You just bought one last week.

A : It's a different color.

A : 雅詩蘭黛的水漾亮彩唇膏在買一送一！我可以買一個大紅色，配一個粉香檳色的。

B : 你上個星期才買了一支。

A : 不同顏色呀！

* two-for-one 買一送一，是 two for the price of one 的簡稱。
* luster lipstick 水潤唇膏。

這種唇蜜很有光亮感。

這句可以這麼說

This lip **glaze** has a **sheen**-style **finish**.

This lip glaze makes the lips super glittery

This lip glaze makes your lips sparkle.

學學老外這麼說

A : How about this lip glaze? It will make you lips super glittery.

B : Should I use it with other types of lipstick?

A : With or without.

A : 這種唇蜜如何？它能讓你的雙唇超級閃亮。

B : 要和其他唇膏一起用嗎？

A : 都可以。

單字

glaze [glez] n.
光亮平滑的表層

sheen [ʃin] n. 光澤

finish [ˈfɪnɪʃ] n.
表面效果

MP3
136

用唇線筆勾勒一下你的唇線。

Use a *lip liner pencil to define the shape of your lips.

Use a lip liner pencil to enhance the shape of your lips.

Outline your lips with a lip liner pencil.

學學老外這麼說

A : What can I do for my thin lips?

B : You can extend your lips to outline a bit with a lip liner pencil.

A : 針對我的薄嘴唇有什麼辦法嗎？

B : 你可以用唇線筆把嘴唇稍微描厚一些。

---

* lip liner pencil 唇線筆。

潤唇膏能滋潤你乾裂的嘴唇。

這句可以這麼說

A *lip balm can moisturize your dry chapped lips.

A lip butter is good for dry chapped lips.

A lip cream helps to heal dry chapped lips.

Your chapped lips need some lipcare.

學學老外這麼說

A : Your lips are dry and chapped. Why don't you apply some lip cream?

B : Me, lipstick?

A : It's not lipstick. Your chapped lips need some lipcare.

B : Anyway, I don't like how it feels on my lips. It's oily and heavy.

A：你的嘴唇又乾又裂，為什麼不塗點潤唇膏？

B：我？塗唇膏？

A：不是唇膏，是潤唇膏，它能滋潤你乾裂的嘴唇。

B：不管怎樣，我不喜歡嘴唇上有油膩膩的厚重感。

---

* lip balm / butter / cream 潤唇膏；護唇膏。

MP3
138

冷霜卸妝很徹底。

***Cold cream** removes makeup thoroughly.

Cold cream is one type of thorough makeup remover.

Cold cream is a very effective makeup remover.

A : What product do you use to remove your makeup thoroughly?

B : Ponds cold cream. It also helps the skin to recover from harsh beauty products.

A : 你用什麼產品來徹底卸妝？

B : 旁氏冷霜，它還能幫助恢復受化妝品摧殘的肌膚。

---

* cold cream 冷霜。

Cold Cream

Little Johnny watched, fascinated, as his mother gently rubbed cold cream on her face.

"Why are you rubbing cold cream on your face, Mommy?" he asked.

"To make myself beautiful," said his mother.

A few minutes later, she began removing the cream with a tissue.

"What's the matter?" asked Little Johnny. "Giving up?"

冷霜

小約翰看著媽媽往臉上輕輕地塗抹冷霜，覺得很有趣。

「媽媽你為什麼要往臉上抹冷霜啊？」他問。

「好讓我變漂亮啊。」媽媽說。

過了幾分鐘，媽媽開始用紙巾擦掉冷霜。

「怎麼了？」小約翰問，「放棄了嗎？」

3 Chapter

美容美髮

三國時，關公刮骨療傷面不改色，今有美女顏面動刀，樂在其中！哈姆雷特名言：「To be or not to be, that is the question.」今有時尚美女猶豫「打肉毒桿菌還是不打肉毒桿菌，這是個問題。（To Botox or not to Botox, that is the question.）」愛美乃人之天性也！時尚美女會定期來個「作臉（facial）」；衝動之下把「大波浪（body wave）」剪成復古「赫本頭（pixie cut）」；沒事就「挑染（highlights）」頭髮改變造型換心情，或是嘗試「脈衝光（photo facial）」。現在她卻自問，是否要挑戰加入「拉皮（face-lift）」、「隆鼻（nose job）」或「漂唇（lip bleaching）」的美容激流中呢？

MP3
139

我約了明天去作臉。

這句可以這麼說

I've made an appointment for a **facial** tomorrow.

I made a facial appointment for tomorrow.

I booked a facial for tomorrow.

學學老外這麼說

A：Wanna grab a beer after work with some friends?

B：I'd like to, but I've made an appointment for a facial.

A：下班和朋友們一起去喝一杯嗎？

B：我很想去，但我約好了要去作臉。

單字
facial [ˋfeʃəl] n.
臉部保養；作臉

MP3
140

你多久作一次臉？

How often do you get a facial?

Do you have a facial regularly?

A : How often should I get a facial?

B : Ideally, every four to six weeks.

A : 我應該多久作一次臉？

B : 最好每四至六個星期一次。

MP3
141

你們有什麼臉部保養的課程？

這句可以這麼說

What facial services do you offer here?

What variety of facials do you provide?

What facial options do you have?

學學老外這麼說

A : What facial services do you offer here?

B : We have the essential facial, mini-facial, and other specialty facials like the **aroma** facial, **herbal** facial, and oxygen facial, etc. Here is our *brochure.

A : 你們有什麼臉部保養的課程？

B : 我們有基本保養、簡易保養，還有特別護理，例如：芳香護理、草藥護理和充氧護理等。這是療程內容。

單字

aroma [ə`romə] adj. 芳香的

herbal [`hɝbl] adj. 草藥的

---

* brochure [bro`ʃur] n. 小手冊；廣告手冊。

我想做除痘和黑頭粉刺的臉部護理。

這句可以這麼說

I want to have a facial to treat my acne and blackheads.

I want to have acne treatment and blackhead extraction.

I need a treatment to prevent ***outbreaks** and extract blackheads.

I want to get rid of my acne and blackheads.

學學老外這麼說

A : How would you like your facial done?

B : I want to have a acne treatment and blackheads extraction.

A : 你想做什麼樣的臉部保養課程？

B : 我想做除痘和黑頭粉刺的療程。

---

* outbreak [`aut͵brek] n. 突然發生。這裡指臉上的青春痘。

MP3
143

我想來個美白護理療程。

這句可以這麼說

I'd like a whitening facial.

I'd like a whitening facial treatment.

I'll go for a specialty facial for skin whitening.

學學老外這麼說

A : We offer a variety of facials. What facial would you like?

B : I'd like a whitening facial.

A : 我們提供各種臉部保養。您想做哪一種？

B : 我想來個美白護理療程。

MP3
144

臉部護理會讓你的皮膚光滑，臉色紅潤。

這句可以這麼說

You'll have smooth skin and rosy cheeks after the facial.

The facial will give you smooth skin and a ruddy complexion.

The facial will make your skin porcelain-like and rosy.

學學老外這麼說

A：Honey, I've just had a facial. How do I look?

B：The facial gives you smooth skin and a ruddy complexion.

A：親愛的，我剛作完臉。看起來如何？

B：臉部護理讓你的皮膚光滑，臉色紅潤。

MP3
145

這家美容院有日晒機嗎？

這句可以這麼說

Are there *tanning beds* in this beauty salon?

Are there tanning booths in this beauty salon?

Does this beauty salon offer a tanning service?

Can I get a tan in this beauty salon?

學學老外這麼說

A：Can I get a tan here?

B：Yes. We have both tanning beds and *spray tanning*.

A：這是家日晒沙龍嗎？

B：是的。我們有日晒床和噴晒設備。

---

* tanning bed / tanning booth 日晒機。

* spray tanning 噴晒。

MP3
146

你打過美白針嗎？

Have you tried whitening injections?

Do you have any experience with whitening injections?

A : I am *fed up with the black spots and freckles on my face. Is there a more efficient whitening recipe than masks?

B : Have you tried whitening injections?

A : 我快被臉上的黑斑和雀斑煩死了。有沒有比敷面膜更快的美白方法？

B : 你打過美白針嗎？

---

* fed up 厭煩，厭倦。

MP3
147

雷射除毛是永久性的嗎？

Is laser ***hair removal** ***permanent**?

Do the effects of laser hair removal last?

A : I am fed up with all the hair removal methods of shaving, plucking, threading and waxing.

B : Laser hair removal is supposed to be permanent.

A : 我厭倦了所有的去毛方法了，不管是刮的、拔的、線拔或蜜蠟除毛。

B : 聽說雷射除毛是永久性的。

---

* hair removal 去體毛。

* permanent [ˋpɝ·mənənt] adj. 永久的。

臉部護理類型

deep-cleansing facial/deep-pore cleansing facial深層清潔臉部護理

　—thorough cleansing 深度清潔

　—skin analysis 肌膚分析

　—exfoliation 去角質

　—extraction of blackheads or whiteheads 去黑頭和白頭粉刺

　—facial massage 臉部按摩

　—a facial mask 面膜

　—application of toners and protective creams 塗保溼水和護膚霜

mini-facial 簡易臉部護理（不含去黑頭過程）

age defense facial 抗老臉部護理

oxygen facial 活氧臉部護理

collagen facial 膠原蛋白滋潤護理

acne facial 抗痘臉部護理

photo facial 脈衝光臉部護理

臉部按摩能抗皺，使皮膚紅潤。

HOPE PLANET SALON

這句可以這麼說

*Facial massage** can prevent wrinkles and create a more reddish and attractive complexion.

Facial massage has anti-wrinkle and skin-glow effects.

學學老外這麼說

A : I like the facial massage when I get a facial. It improves my blood circulation and relaxes my skin.

B : Why don't you get yourself a facial **massager**?

A : 我喜歡作臉時來個臉部按摩，可以抗皺，使皮膚紅潤。

B : 那就買個臉部按摩器吧？

單字

massager
[mə`sɑʒɚ] n.
按摩器

---

* facial massage 臉部按摩。

196

這家 spa 館按摩技術不錯。

這句可以這麼說

This **spa** offers very good ***massage therapy**.

This spa is well known for its massage therapy.

This spa has really good massage therapists.

I recommend the massage therapy at this spa.

學學老外這麼說

A：I am really exhausted. My back is killing me.

B：Why don't you go for a spa treatment downstairs?
　　Their massage therapists are really good.

A：我快累癱了。我的背痛死了。

B：你去樓下店裡做個水療如何？他們的按摩師手法很不錯。

單字

spa [spɑ] n.
水療

* massage therapy 按摩療法。

197

MP3
150

足療多少錢？

這句可以這麼說

How much do you charge for a **pedicure**?

How much do I owe you for the pedicure?

How much is it for a pedicure?

學學老外這麼說

A : How much do I owe you?

B : 20 dollars. 10 dollars for the foot massage and 10 dollars for a pedicure.

A : 多少錢？

B : 二十美元。腳底按摩十塊，足療十塊。

單字
pedicure
[ˋpɛdɪ.kjur] n.
足療；修腳

MP3
151

刮痧能治療中暑。

這句可以這麼說

*Skin scraping** can cure **sunstroke**.

Skin scraping is a treatment for sunstroke.

Skin scraping really works for sunstroke.

學學老外這麼說

A : I want to try skin scraping. What do you think?

B : It does cure sunstroke. But it leaves large **bruises** on the skin.

A : I've heard it improves blood circulation and your skintone.

A : 我想試試刮痧，你覺得如何？

B : 刮痧確實能治中暑，但在皮膚上會留下大塊瘀青。

A : 我還聽說它能改善血液循環和膚色。

單字

sunstroke
[`sʌn.strok] n. 中暑

bruise [bruz] n.
瘀青

* skin scraping 刮痧。

拔罐疼不疼啊？

Traditional Chinese Medicine

這句可以這麼說

Does **cupping** hurt?

Is cupping painful?

學學老外這麼說

A：I notice you offer cupping treatments here. Does it hurt?

B：It may hurt during the treatment. But it can cure back pain.

A：我發現你們這裡有拔罐治療，會痛嗎？

B：拔的時候會有點痛，但它能治背痛。

單字

cupping [ˋkʌpɪŋ]
n. 拔罐

Energizing Facial Massage DIY 提神臉部按摩DIY

中醫美容已經征服了西方人，按摩也不再是亞洲人的最愛，美容院裡也有了按摩、刮痧或拔罐等專業服務，特別是「臉部按摩（facial massage）」，已經成為歐式臉部護理美容的一個不可缺少的項目。下面提供一招臉部提神按摩 DIY：

Make yourself comfortable. （調整到自己舒服的姿勢。）

Tap your scalp with your fingertips for one minute. （用指尖輕敲頭皮一分鐘。）

Hold your hands flat and move your head back and forth 10 times, rubbing your forehead on your hands. （手平放於額前，透過頭部晃動用掌心摩擦前額十次。）

Circling your eyes with your knuckles 10 times. （用指關節按摩眼圈十次。）

Rub your cheeks with your palms 10 times. （用掌心畫圓按摩臉頰十次。）

Hold your hands flat and move your head back and forth 10 times, rubbing your mouth on your hands. （手平放於嘴上，透過頭部晃動使掌心摩擦嘴巴十次。）

Pull the skin on your throat 10 times with your hands. （用手輕拉頸部皮膚十次。）

Massage your ears. Separate your hands like the Vulcan greeting and rub around the ears, and then massage the cartilage and lobes. （手指分開，無名指和小拇指併攏，中指和食指併攏，耳朵於其間摩擦，之後按摩耳骨和耳垂。）

MP3
153

你經常去做 spa 嗎?

這句可以這麼說

Do you often go to spas?

Do you have spa treatments regularly?

How often do you go to spas?

學學老外這麼說

A : Do you often go to spas?

B : Once a month to a day spa. But I really want to spend some quality time at a destination spa or a resort spa.

A : 你經常去做 spa 嗎?

B : 一個月做一次都會型 spa,但我真的很想花點時間去做個主題 spa 或度假村型 spa。

MP3 154

這種熱泉 spa 有美容功效。

這句可以這麼說

This ***thermal spa** has beautifying effects.

This thermal spa refreshes and recharges your skin.

This thermal spa works better than cosmetics.

學學老外這麼說

A：This thermal spa is as good as skin care products.

B：Really? I'll give it a try.

A：這種熱泉 spa 有美容功效。

B：真的嗎？我要試試。

* thermal [ˋθɝml] adj. 熱的；溫泉的。thermal spa 熱泉 spa。

spa 有助於舒壓、放鬆身心。

───《 這句可以這麼說 》───

Spa treatment helps to relieve stress and relax your body.

You can relax your mind and body by having a spa.

Hydrotherapy has relaxing and stress-relieving effects.

───《 學學老外這麼說 》───

A : This is really refreshing.

B : Spa treatment can relax your mind and body.

A : 真是讓人心曠神怡。

B : spa 有助舒壓、放鬆身心。

單字

hydrotherapy
[ˌhaɪdrəˋθɛrəpɪ] n.
水療

MP3
156

這家 spa 館很輕鬆、安靜。

I like the relaxing and quiet atmosphere of this spa.
This spa has a relaxing, quiet and calming ambiance.
This spa offers a retreat from the noisy daily life.

A : This spa has a relaxing, quiet and calming
  ambiance.
B : Yeah, I don't like to go to a busy one.
A : 這家 spa 館很輕鬆、安靜。
B : 我也覺得，我不喜歡去那種人多的 spa 館。

MP3
157

這家 spa 館不夠乾淨。

這句可以這麼說

This spa is not clean enough.

The **sanitation** at this spa is not good enough.

This spa is unsanitary.

學學老外這麼說

A : This spa is unsanitary. I'd like it better if it were super clean.

B : Yeah. They never change the **ratty** towels and robes, they don't take out the trash, and they don't fix the broken sinks.

A : 這家 spa 館不夠衛生。如果很乾淨，我就會喜歡它。

B : 是啊，毛巾和袍子破舊不堪也不換，垃圾滿了也不倒，水槽壞了也不修。

單字

sanitation
[͵sænəˋteʃən] n.
衛生設施；環境衛生

ratty [ˋrætɪ] adj.
（口）破舊的；破爛的

本店會員打八折。

這句可以這麼說

We offer a *discount rate of 20% with membership.

Our **parlor** gives a 20% discount to members.

Members of our parlor enjoy all the treatments at a 20% discount rate.

All the treatments in our parlor are 20% off for members.

學學老外這麼說

A : Does the spa have discounts or *special offers for membership?

B : Yes. All the treatments in our parlor are 20% off for members.

A : 那家 spa 館有沒有會員打折或者特價優惠？

B : 有的。會員打八折。

單字

discount
[ˋdɪskaunt] n. 折扣；打折

parlor [ˋpɑrlɚ] n. 店

---

* 注意英語的 20% discount 或者 20% off 指的是八折優惠。

* special offer 特價優惠。

可以從這家 spa 館的網站列印優惠券。

這句可以這麼說

This spa offers printable **coupons** on its website.

You can print out coupons from the spa center's website.

You can get some printable coupons from the spa center website.

學學老外這麼說

A : Do you have any discounts?

B : Yes. You can print out coupons from our website.

A：你們有打折嗎？

B：有，可以從我們的網站上列印優惠券。

單字
coupon [`kjupan]
n. 優惠券；折價券

spa 的種類

源自於拉丁文「Solus Par Aqua」，意為「藉由水舒展身心、獲得健康」。西方人所說的 spa 包含有相當的心靈平衡含意，如今 spa 已經融合了美容、健身和養生等概念，而且發展出不同的類型，但不論哪種 spa，共同點都是讓顧客們放鬆身心，恢復活力。

「一日型 spa／都會型 spa（day spa／city spa）」一般和美容院結合，提供一個小時到一整天的美容，按摩和水療等服務，不提供住宿。

「主題型 spa（destination spa）」主要是透過美容、水療、健身以及養生美容課程，讓顧客的生活方式變得健康，需要住宿三到七天，至少兩個晚上。

「度假村型 spa（resort spa）」滿足顧客綜合性的度假需求，除美容、水療和保健，還提供如高爾夫、滑雪，以及兒童娛樂等各種娛樂項目。

另外還有「醫學 spa（medical spa）」，除了提供普通美容和水療外，還有醫生提供「肉毒桿菌（Botox）」和「雷射美容（laser surfacing）」等服務。

「礦質溫泉 spa（mineral springs spa）」提供天然的礦物泉，用溫泉或海水作「水療（hydrotherapy）」。

你需要修眉嗎？

這句可以這麼說

Do you need your eyebrows done?

Would you like an eyebrow shaping treatment?

Would you like your eyebrows groomed?

學學老外這麼說

A：Do you need your eyebrows done?

B：Yes. Do you do *eye threading here? I've heard that could last 3 to 4 weeks.

A：Yes. You will find it gives you a very clean brow line.

A：你需要修眉嗎？

B：好的。你們做挽眉嗎？我聽說這種方法能保持三到四個星期。

A：有，你會發現拔過之後，眉線會變得很乾淨。

---

* eye threading 挽眉法。

紋眉好還是繡眉好？

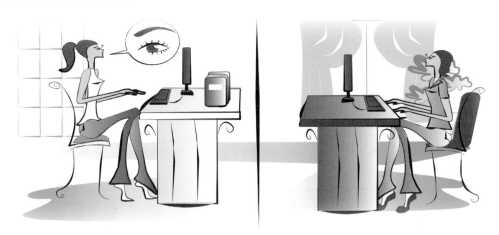

這句可以這麼說

*Eyebrow tattooing, or *eyebrow embroidery?

Are you going to go for eyebrow tattooing, or eyebrow embroidery?

Does eyebrow tattooing look more natural than eyebrow embroidery, or vice versa?

學學老外這麼說

A : I can't decide whether to have my eyebrows tattooed or eyebrows embroidered.

B : I don't know the difference between the two, and I suggest neither. Can't you just use some eyebrow powder every day?

A : 我無法決定到底要紋眉還是繡眉。

B : 我不知道兩者有什麼區別，也不贊成任何一種。你就不能每天用點眉粉嗎？

---

* eyebrow tattooing 紋眉。

* eyebrow embroidery 繡眉。

MP3 162

你的眉形不太適合你的臉型。

這句可以這麼說

The shape of your eyebrows doesn't match the shape of your face.

The shape of your eyebrows doesn't suit your face.

Your brow lines don't flatter your face.

學學老外這麼說

A : I just had my eyebrows groomed in the beauty salon.

B : That round *halolike shape makes your round face even rounder. It doesn't suit you.

A : 我剛去美容院把我的眉毛修了一下。

B : 這種圓弧形的柳葉眉讓你的臉看起來更圓，真的不適合你。

---

* halo [`helo] n. 指「（聖人頭頂上的）光環；光輪」。

眉形與臉型

The "perfect" brow shape, the soft angled shape, works beautifully with an oval face shape. （完美眉形，柔和圓弧眉形，最適合鵝蛋臉。）

A high arched brow makes a round face appear longer and less round. （高挑眉使圓臉看起來較不圓，有把臉拉長的效果。）

A flat brow shape makes a long face shape appear shorter. （一字眉能使長臉型變短。）

Angled brows soften the strong jaw line of a square face shape. （圓弧形眉軟化方形臉的強硬下巴線條。）

A low-arch round browline creates a natural look for a heart shaped face and is soft, feminine, and attractive. （小弧度的弓形眉配心形臉顯得自然，而且具有柔和女性的魅力美。）

臉型和髮型 (1)

oval

Try: A variety of styles, especially slicked-backed looks.

Avoid: Hairstyles covering up your face or heavy bangs.

鵝蛋臉

嘗試：各種髮型適用，特別推薦順梳到腦後的髮型。

避免：擋住臉型的髮型，或是厚重的瀏海。

heart shaped

Try: Chin-length or longer styles, especially a chin length bob. Avoid: Short, full styles that emphasize the upper face.

心形臉

嘗試：下巴長度或稍長髮型，特別推薦下巴長度的鮑伯頭。

避免：又短又豐厚的髮型，突出臉的上半部。

去光水用多了指甲會變脆弱。

這句可以這麼說

Frequent use of *nail polish remover* makes your nails fragile.

Your nails may chap if you use too much nail polish remover.

Nail polish remover may make your nails chapped.

學學老外這麼說

A : I want to change my nail polish every day.

B : You should use nail polish remover once a week at most, or your nails will chap easily.

A : 我想每天換不同顏色的指甲油。

B : 你應該一個星期最多用一次去光水，否則你的指甲會很容易脆裂。

---

* nail polish remover 去光水。

MP3
164

假指甲對身體有害。

***False nails** are not good for your health.

False nails do lots of damage to your nails.

False nails are not healthy.

A : Should I wear false nails or nail polish?

B : False nails are even less healthy than nail polish.

A : 我該戴假指甲還是塗指甲油呢？

B : 假指甲比指甲油更不健康。

---

* false nail 假指甲。

Film Star

A witch went into a beauty parlor and asked the assistant how much it would cost to make her look like a film star. "Nothing," replied the assistant. "Nothing?" she asked, "but how can I look like a film star?" "Haven't you seen a film called *The Creature from the Black Lagoon*?" replied the assistant.

電影明星

一個女巫去美容院，詢問假如要有像電影明星一樣的容貌得花多少錢。「不用錢，」美容助理回答。「不用錢？」她問，「那我要怎樣才能像電影明星？」「你沒看過有部電影叫『黑湖妖潭』嗎？」助理回答。

MP3
165

我的頭髮很毛燥。

這句可以這麼說

My hair is quite coarse.

My hair is so dull.

My hair is too rough.

My hair feels like straw.

學學老外這麼說

A : My hair is so dull. **Conditioners** don't work. What can I do?

B : You can try some *deep charge treatment, or *hair spa or *hair mask products.

A : 我的頭髮很毛燥。護髮乳也不管用。怎麼辦？

B : 你可以試試深層護髮、水療式按摩洗髮，或者用髮膜。

---

* deep charge treatment 護髮。

* hair spa 水療式按摩洗髮。

* hair mask 髮膜。

單字

conditioner
[kən`dɪʃənɚ] n.
護髮乳

217

MP3
166

怎麼處理我的自然捲？

這句可以這麼說

What can I do with my ***frizzy hair**?

How can I tame my puffy hair?

Is there any way to handle my uncontrollable, bulky hair?

學學老外這麼說

A：How can I tame my puffy hair?

B：You can have it straightened or permed.

A：怎麼處理我的自然捲？

B：你可以燙直或燙捲。

---

* frizzy / puffy hair 捲曲散亂的頭髮

怎麼樣可以讓頭髮看起來蓬鬆又自然？

這句可以這麼說

How can I make my hair puffy and natural?

How can I add some natural volume to my hair?

學學老外這麼說

A：My hair is too flat on the top. How can I make my hair puffy and natural?

B：Apply some *mousse and *blow dry your hair upside down.

A：我頭頂上的頭髮太塌了，怎麼讓頭髮可以蓬鬆又自然？

B：抹點慕絲，然後頭朝下吹乾頭髮。

單字
mousse [mus] n. 慕絲

---

* mousse 原指「有泡沫的奶油甜點」；這裡指的是泡沫狀的髮膠。

* blow dry 吹乾。

MP3
168

我頭髮掉得厲害。

這句可以這麼說

My hair keeps falling out.

My hair is **thinning**.

My **hairline** is **receding**.

I am suffering from hair loss.

學學老外這麼說

A : My hair keeps falling out since the **perm**.

B : Don't worry. It will grow back in.

A：燙過頭髮以後我的頭髮掉得厲害。

B：別擔心，你的頭髮會重新長出來的。

單字

thin [θɪn] v.
變得稀疏

hairline [ˋhɛr͵laɪn]
n. 髮際線；非常細
的線條

recede [rɪˋsid] v.
向後傾斜；（頭頂
前部髮線）後移

220

A Strange Woman

When a new perm turned out to be a disaster, I phoned my husband and issued a one-line warning: "Don't say anything about my hair." During dinner, we discussed the weather, his day at the office—anything but my hair. I began to feel uneasy. Finally, when we were washing the dishes, he said in a serious tone, "You'd better go now. My wife will be here any moment, and she wouldn't like to find me with a strange woman."

一個陌生女人

我去燙頭髮，結果燙得很失敗。於是我打了個電話警告我的丈夫：「不要對我的頭髮發表任何評論。」吃飯的時候，我們聊天氣，聊他一天的工作——完全不談我的頭髮。我開始有些不安了。最後，在我們洗碗的時候，他非常認真地說：「你得走了。我太太隨時都會回來，她看到我和一個陌生女人在一起會不高興的。」

MP3
169

我想去剪頭髮。

這句可以這麼說

I'd like to have my hair cut.

I need a haircut.

I need to go to the *hairdressers.

I need to go to the *hair salon.

I need to get my hair done.

學學老外這麼說

A : I'd like to have my hair cut. Do you know any good
hairdressers?

B : Punk Hairdressers is not bad.

A : 我想去剪頭髮，你覺得哪家美髮院比較好？

B : 龐克美髮店不錯。

---

* 除了 hairdressers，另有 barber's 男性理髮店，barber 指男性理髮師（幫男
性理髮及刮鬍子）。

* hair salon 美髮沙龍。

單字

hairdressers
['hɛr,drɛsəs] 美髮院

MP3
170

你有指定的設計師嗎?

這句可以這麼說

Do you have your own *hair stylist?
Which hair stylist do you prefer?
Which hairdresser do you like?

學學老外這麼說

A : Do you have your own hair stylist?
B : No.
A : May I recommend one of our best stylists?
B : Yes, please.
A : 你有指定的髮型設計師嗎?
B : 沒有。
A : 那我推薦我們最好的髮型設計師,好嗎?
B : 好的,麻煩你。

---

* hair stylist 髮型設計師。

MP3
171

你平時綁頭髮嗎？

這句可以這麼說

Do you wear your hair up or down?

How do you usually wear your hair?

學學老外這麼說

A : How do you usually wear your hair?

B : I usually do it up in a ***bun** or ***ponytail**. My company has strict hair codes.

A : 你平常都是什麼髮型？

B : 我都把頭髮盤起來梳成髻或綁馬尾。我們公司對髮型的要求很嚴格。

---

* bun [bʌn] n. 圓髮髻。

* ponytail [ˋponɪˌtel] n. 馬尾（指頭髮）。另有 pigtail，指的是將頭髮編成辮子。

MP3
172

你想要什麼髮型？

How would you like your hair done?

How do you want your hair?

What kind of hairstyle would you like?

Which hair style would you prefer?

學學老外這麼說

A : How would you like your hair done?

B : My hair is a bit too thick in the back. Can you *thin it **out** without changing my hairstyle?

A : Sure.

A : 你想要什麼髮型？

B : 我後面的頭髮很厚。能幫我打薄但不要改變髮型嗎？

A : 沒問題。

---

* thin out 使變薄（thining scissors 打薄）。

我只想修一下頭髮。

這句可以這麼說

I'd like a *trim.

A trim will do.

Just a trim, please.

Can you give my hair a good trimming?

學學老外這麼說

A : How would you like your hair cut?

B : A trim will do. A little off the top, but not too much
at the back.

A : 你想剪什麼髮型？

B : 修一下就行。頭頂稍微剪一點，但後面不要剪得太多。

---

* trim [trɪm] n. 修剪；修髮尾。

我想換個新髮型。

這句可以這麼說

I'd like a new **hairdo**.

I am ready for a new hairdo.

I want to change my hair style.

學學老外這麼說

A：Do you want to keep your old style or a new one?

B：I'd like a new hairdo.

A：你想保持原來的髮型，還是換個新造型？

B：我想換個新髮型。

單字

hairdo [`hɛr͵du]
n.（口）（尤指女子）髮型；做頭髮

227

你的頭髮要剪短嗎？

這句可以這麼說

Would you like it a little shorter?
Do you prefer a shorter hair style?

學學老外這麼說

A：Do you prefer a shorter hair style?
B：Yes, I prefer it short.
A：你的頭髮要剪短嗎？
B：是的，我喜歡短髮。

MP3
176

我剛做了接髮。

這句可以這麼說

I just got *hair extensions.

I've just had hair extensions done.

學學老外這麼說

A : Are you wearing a **wig**? I remember you had short hair yesterday.

B : Haven't you heard about hair extensions?

A : 你戴了假髮嗎？我記得你昨天是短頭髮。

B : 你沒聽說過接髮嗎？

單字

wig [wɪg] n. 假髮

---

* hair extension 接髮。

瀏海怎麼剪？

這句可以這麼說

How would you like your **fringe**?

How would you like your **bangs**?

學學老外這麼說

A : How would you like your bangs?

B : *Wispy bangs look better with my face.

A : 你的瀏海想留齊還是打薄？

B : 打薄瀏海比較適合我的臉型。

單字

fringe [frɪndʒ]
n.（英）瀏海

bangs [bæŋs]
n.（美）瀏海

---

* wispy bangs 不對稱打薄的瀏海。chopped bangs 指的是整齊的瀏海。

MP3
178

你能替我做照片上的髮型嗎？

Can you do my hair like this picture?

Can you cut it like the hair in this picture?

Can you make my hair look like this?

A : Can you make my hair look like this picture?

B : Actually, this hairstyle doesn't suit you. It will
exaggerate your round face.

A : 你能幫我做照片上的這種髮型嗎？

B : 事實上，這個髮型不太適合你，它會讓你的臉看起來更圓。

髮型

crew cut / crop 平頭

shoulder length hair 披肩長髮

curly hair 鬈髮

straight hair 直髮

wavy hair 大波浪

bun / knot 髮髻

chaplet （戴在頭上的）花冠狀髮飾

pig-tail(s) 豬尾巴髮型（頭髮紮成一或兩股垂在背後或兩肩）

braided 麻花辮

pony-tail 馬尾

bob 鮑伯頭

pixie cut 赫本頭

pageboy style 娃娃頭（髮梢全部向內捲）

Afro 爆炸頭

Mohawk 龐克頭（兩側剃短只留中間部分，且抹上髮膠使頭髮豎起）

Dreadlocks 雷鬼頭（牙買加拉斯塔法理人滿頭又細又長的辮子）

洗頭加做頭髮一共多少錢？

這句可以這麼說

How much do you charge for a shampoo and set?

How much is a shampoo and set?

How much do I owe you for the shampoo and set?

學學老外這麼說

A : How much is a shampoo and set?

B : 50 dollars.

A : 洗頭加做頭髮一共多少錢？

B : 五十塊美金。

單字

set [sɛt] n.
固定髮型；做頭髮

MP3
180

這種髮型非常適合你的臉型。

這句可以這麼說

This hairstyle really flatters your face.

This hairstyle is perfect for the shape of your face.

學學老外這麼說

A : Are there any new styles lately?

B : How about this cute *pageboy style in the picture?
This hairstyle is perfect for the shape of your face.

A : 最近有什麼新的髮型？

B : 這張圖片上的可愛娃娃頭你覺得怎麼樣？這種髮型非常適合你的臉
型。

---

* pageboy [`pedʒ͵bɔɪ] n. 行李員，男侍從。

MP3
181

我的新髮型好看嗎？

這句可以這麼說

Do you like my new hairstyle?

Do you like my new hairdo?

How do you like my new hairstyle?

What do you think of my new hairstyle?

學學老外這麼說

A : How do you like my new hairdo?

B : It's great. It highlights your oval face.

A：我的新髮型好看嗎？

B：很漂亮，和你的鵝蛋臉很搭。

你的新髮型真漂亮！

這句可以這麼說

What a great new hairstyle!

You look good with your new hairstyle.

I like your hair.

I love your new hairstyle!

學學老外這麼說

A：What a great new hairstyle! It really suits you.

B：Thank you!

A：你的新髮型真迷人！真的很適合你呢。

B：謝謝！

臉型和髮型 (2)

round

Try: Sleek lines and tapered ends, especially pixie cuts or wild tousled styles.

Avoid: Chin length hair with a rounded line, center parts, short crops, or straight "chopped" bangs.

圓臉

嘗試：光亮平滑髮型和削髮（尾部漸細），特別推薦赫本頭（分層次的女短髮）和凌亂蓬鬆的髮型。

避免：下巴長度的圓形外緣髮型、中分、平頭、整齊的瀏海。

long

Try: Bangs, layers, curls and waves, especially chin-length bobs.

Avoid: Too short or too long hair.

長臉

嘗試：瀏海、有層次、鬈髮和波浪造型，特別推薦下巴長度的鮑伯頭。

避免：頭髮過長或過短。

Square

Try: Curls, waves, wispy bangs, especially off-center parts with height at the crown.

Avoid：Chin-length hair, long straight styles, straight bangs or center parts.

方臉

嘗試：鬈髮、大波浪、不對稱瀏海，特別推薦旁分的厚重髮型。

避免：下巴長度髮型、長直髮型、直瀏海和中分頭。

03 人造美女

MP3 183

身體哪些部位可以抽脂？

Plastic Surgery Clinic

這句可以這麼說

Which body parts are usually targeted for **liposuction**?

On which parts of my body can I get liposuction done?

Which body parts can be **suctioned**?

學學老外這麼說

A：Which body parts can be suctioned?

B：Almost any body part could be liposuctioned.
For example, the chin, cheeks, upper arms, chest,
tummy, thighs, ***saddlebags**, back, ***love handles**, and
legs.

A：身體哪些部位可以抽脂？

B：幾乎任何部位都可以抽脂。例如：下巴、臉頰、上臂、胸部、腹
部、大腿、大腿外側、背部、肋腹和腿部。

單字

liposuction
[ˋlaɪpoˌsʌkʃən] n.
脂肪抽吸術

suction [ˋsʌkʃən]
n. 抽吸

* saddle bag [ˋsæd!ˌbæg] n. 大腿外側上方肥肉；鞍囊。

* love handle，就是俗稱的游泳圈。

我想除掉我的雙下巴。

這句可以這麼說

I want to get rid of my *double chin.

I am going to get my double chin removed.

How I wish I could lose my double chin!

How I wish that my double chin would disappear!

學學老外這麼說

A : How I wish that my double chin would disappear!

B : You can try liposuction.

A : 我好想讓我的雙下巴消失啊！

B : 你可以試試抽脂。

---

* double chin 雙下巴。

MP3
185

我的象腿讓我很痛苦。

這句可以這麼說

My *thunder thighs make me sad.

My thunder thighs really bother me.

I hate my huge thighs.

學學老外這麼說

A : I hate my thunder thighs.

B : If it really bothers you, you can have liposuction done.

A : 我討厭我的象腿。

B : 如果真的讓你很困擾，你就去抽脂吧！

---

* thunder thighs 此處指肥胖的腿，醫學上也有較少見的象腿病。

抽脂後，我穿無袖衣服好看多了。

這句可以這麼說

Since the liposuction, I look better wearing **sleeveless** shirts.

I can wear sleeveless shirts again since the liposuction.

Liposuction makes me look better in sleeveless shirts.

學學老外這麼說

A : How about this tank top? Want to try it on?

B : Of course! Since the liposuction, I look better wearing sleeveless shirts.

A : 這件坦克背心如何？想試試看嗎？

B : 當然！抽脂後，我穿無袖衣服好看多了。

單字

sleeveless
[`slivlɪs] adj. 無袖的

告別「游泳圈」。

這句可以這麼說

No more *spare tire*.

Say goodbye to your *muffin top*.

Get rid of your love handles permanently.

Keep your thin waist.

學學老外這麼說

A：How can I get rid of my love handles?

B：If you can't maintain an exercise routine, then your only choice is liposuction.

A：要怎樣做才能消掉我的游泳圈呢？

B：如果你不能持續運動，那就只能做抽脂了。

---

* spare tire 備用輪胎，這裡指的是腰部贅肉。

* muffin top 肚腩肉（澳洲近年自創的字詞）。muffin 原為「瑪芬」（一種點心）。

做腹部拉皮或是多運動？

這句可以這麼說

Tummytuck, or more exercise?

Should I try a tummytuck, or get more exercise?

Which should I choose, a tummytuck or more exercise?

How can I get a flat stomach, with a tummytuck or more exercise?

學學老外這麼說

A：I really envy her flat stomach!

B：Me too! Maybe I should try a tummytuck or get more exercise.

A：我好羨慕她平坦的小腹。

B：我也是！也許我該去做腹部拉皮或多運動！

單字

tummytuck
[ˋtʌmɪtʌk] n.
腹部拉皮；縮腹手術

胖子胖在哪裡？

double chin 雙下巴

bra fat 穿胸罩周邊擠出的肥肉

flabby arms 蝴蝶袖、掰掰肉

pot belly 大肚腩（一般指男子）

menopot 更年期肥肉

love handles / muffin top / spare tire 腰腹游泳圈

saddle bags 大腿外側上方肥肉

thunder thighs 象腿

另外說人胖的用詞褒貶要準確，不要得罪胖子哦！

flabby 肥胖而肌肉鬆垮不結實，貶意高。

pudgy 短胖的、短粗的，常指手指和手，貶意高。

obese 過度肥胖的、胖的呈病態的人，貶意。

fat 肥胖的（最常用且最直接），貶意。

overweight 超重的、肥胖的，中性。

chubby 圓胖可愛的、稍胖的，常指嬰兒的臉。

stout 粗壯結實的、身體胖得勻稱，褒意低。

tubby 矮胖的、含親切感，褒意低。

plump 稍胖或豐滿，褒意低。

MP3 189

你想做隆乳手術嗎？

這句可以這麼說

Are you going to have breast **augmentation** surgery?

Will you get breast **implants**?

Do you want to get a **boob** job?

學學老外這麼說

A : Will you get breast implants?

B : No. I can't imagine silicone implants in my body.

A : 你會想做隆乳手術嗎？

B : 不會。我無法想像在體內植入矽膠的感覺。

單字

augmentation
[ˌɔgmɛnˋteʃən] n.
增大；增加

implant [ɪmˋplænt]
n. 植入物

boobs [bubs]
n.（俚）乳房

有什麼天然豐胸的方法嗎？

這句可以這麼說

How to **boost** my **bust** naturally?

Is there a natural way to increase my bust?

Is there an alternative to plastic surgery that can increase my cup size?

How can I increase my cup size without having surgery?

學學老外這麼說

A：How can I increase my cup size without having surgery?

B：You can try massage and acupuncture.

A：有什麼天然豐胸的方法？

B：你可以試試按摩和針灸。

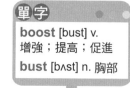

單字

boost [bust] v.
增強；提高；促進

bust [bʌst] n. 胸部

這種豐胸液根本沒有作用。

這句可以這麼說

This *bust beauty serum** doesn't work.

This bust beauty serum is useless.

This bust beauty serum is rubbish.

This bust beauty serum makes no difference.

學學老外這麼說

A : I just bought this bust beauty serum.

B : These products make no difference.

A : 我剛買了這種豐胸液。

B : 這些東西根本沒有用。

---

* bust beauty serum 豐胸液。

美胸五招

豐胸不一定非要靠手術和吃藥,如果不願意花心思做豐胸按摩或塗抹豐胸液,那就試試這五招,馬上見效:

❶ 「矽膠胸貼」或「乳貼」(jelly inserts /chicken cutlets / falsies)現在大行其道,甚至男星也開始使用

❷ 「水胸罩」(water bras)柔順塑型

❸ 「魔力胸罩」(miracle bras)打造挺拔身姿

❹ 「V領襯衣」(V neck shirts)襯托乳溝

❺ 「閃光粉或凡士林」(shimmer or vaseline)露乳溝時反光顯形

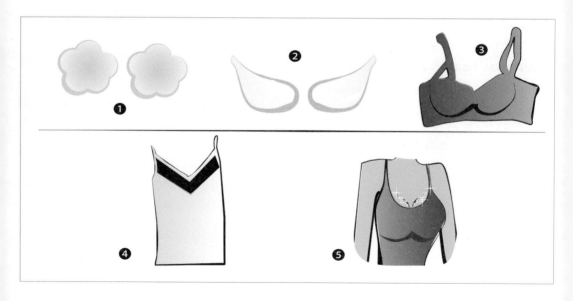

MP3
192

很多名人定期做脈衝光。

這句可以這麼說

Many celebrities have regular *IPL treatments.
Many celebrities get photo facials regularly.

學學老外這麼說

A : Look at her baby smooth skin!
B : She goes to the beauty salon for photo facials
    regularly.

A : 看她的皮膚，像嬰兒般光滑。

B : 她定期去美容院做脈衝光。

---

* IPL = intense pulse light photo facial 脈衝光，簡稱 IPL 或 photo facial。

MP3
193

你聽過微晶煥膚術嗎？

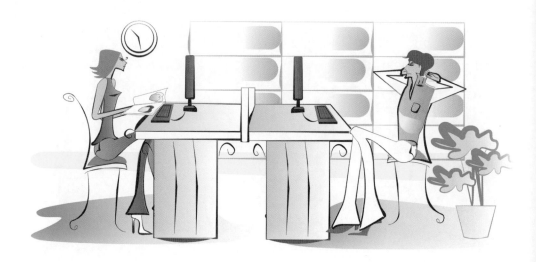

━━ **這句可以這麼說** ━━

Have you heard about *microdermabrasion?

Do you know about microdermabrasion?

What do you know about microdermabrasion?

━━ **學學老外這麼說** ━━

A : What do you know about microdermabrasion?

B : It improves skin tone, softens, and polishes away
mild sun damage, scars, and wrinkles.

A : 你知道微晶煥膚術嗎？

B : 微晶煥膚術可以改善膚色、軟化膚質以及除去晒傷皮膚、疤痕和臉
上皺紋。

---

* microdermabrasion[ˋmaɪkroˌdɚməˋbreʒən] 微晶煥膚術，簡稱
microderm。

MP3
194

她剛做了臉部拉皮。

這句可以這麼說

She just had a ***face-lift**.
She just got a face-lift.

學學老外這麼說

A : The model doesn't look natural. Her face is kind of fake.
B : You know, she may have had a face-lift, or an eye-lift.

A : 這個模特兒看起來不太自然，她的臉有點假假的。
B : 看得出來，她可能做過臉部拉皮，或者眼部拉皮。

---

* face-lift 整容手術，臉部拉皮手術。

MP3
195

肉毒桿菌能除皺。

Botox can prevent wrinkles.

Botox can reduce wrinkles.

Botox can keep your face wrinkle-free.

Botox smooths your wrinkles.

Botox is a good cure for wrinkles.

A : Can Botox really reduce wrinkles?

B : Yes. It can make you look younger for a period of time.

A : 肉毒桿菌真的能除皺嗎？

B : 對，它能讓你在一段時間內看起來更年輕。

單字
Botox [`botaks] n. 肉毒桿菌（注射肉毒桿菌可以達到除皺及瘦臉的功效）

MP3 196

你贊成打肉毒桿菌還是做臉部針灸？

這句可以這麼說

Are you in favor of Botox or *facial acupuncture?

Do you favor Botox or cosmetic acupuncture?

Do you side with Botox or facial acupuncture?

Are you for Botox or facial acupuncture?

學學老外這麼說

A：Are you for Botox or facial acupuncture?

B：Facial acupuncture, though I don't know if it works or is just a myth.

A：你贊成打肉毒桿菌還是做臉部針灸？

B：臉部針灸，雖然不知道它到底管不管用。

---

* facial acupuncture / cosmetic acupuncture 臉部針灸。

永遠的抗老戰爭

女人最怕什麼？歲月的痕跡。這場抗老戰爭，從二十五歲開始就永無休止。

Anti aging / anti wrinkle skin care products. （抗老 / 抗皺護膚品。）

Age defying cosmetic surgery including facelifts, Botox treatments. （抗老美容手術包括整容、打肉毒桿菌。）

Anti-aging and longevity products and supplements--DHA, Estrogen, HGH. （抗老和延壽產品及補品，如卵磷脂、雌激素、生長激素。）

Regular caloric restriction and moderate exercise. （每日限制卡路里攝取量，並適度運動。）

眼睛的類別

almond eyes 杏眼

round eyes 圓眼

deep-set eyes 深窩眼

hooded eyes 厚眼皮眼

bulging / prominent eyes 凸眼（金魚眼）

turned down eyes 垂眼（下斜眼）

puffy eyes 泡泡眼

wide-set eyes 遠心眼（雙眼內眥間距過寬）

close-set eyes 近心眼（雙眼內眥間距過窄）

她做了雙眼皮手術。

這句可以這麼說

She just got her eyelids done with *plastic surgery.
She just had *double eyelid surgery.

學學老外這麼說

A：Look at my eyes, sweetheart!

B：What did you *getting at?

A：I had double eyelid surgery. Can't you see the difference?

A：親愛的，看著我的眼睛！

B：你在暗示什麼啊？

A：我割了雙眼皮。你看不出差別嗎？

---

* plastic surgery 整型手術。
* double eyelid 雙眼皮。
* get at（俚）暗示。

我的眼皮下垂。

這句可以這麼說

My eyelids are **drooping**.

I have droopy eyelids.

I have drooping eyelids.

學學老外這麼說

A : My eyelids are drooping. Do you do eyelid reshaping surgery?

B : Yes. But is it because of Botox? If yes, it will be better after about 1 month or so.

A : 我的眼皮下垂。你們有做眼皮手術嗎？

B : 有。但你是不是打了肉毒桿菌？如果是的話，大概一個月後就會好些。

單字

droop [drup] v. 下垂

256

MP3
199

小眼睛能做手術變大眼睛。

Eyelid improvement may turn small eyes into big eyes.

Small eyes can be "opened up" by cosmetic surgery.

Plastic surgery may "open up" small eyes.

You can make small eyes larger with plastic surgery.

A : She's got really beautiful big eyes!

B : I heard her eyes were opened up through eyelid
surgery. Plastic surgery may "open up" small eyes.

A : 她的大眼睛真漂亮！

B : 我聽說她的眼睛做過眼皮手術。小眼睛能做手術變大眼睛。

257

我想做去眼袋手術。

I want to try the *eyebag removal surgery.

I want to have my eyebags removed.

I'd like to have an *eye lift operation.

I want to have the bags under my eyes removed.

A : What can you do for mature and crinkly eyes?

B : We offer eye lift operation.

A : 你們有什麼辦法對付衰老多皺紋的眼睛?

B : 我們有提供眼部拉提手術。

---

* eyebag removal surgery 除眼袋手術。

* eye lift 眼部拉提。

Risks vs. Rewards 風險與回報

人造美女已經不再是新鮮事，整型已經成為美容的一部分，是一個大眾化的議題。在眾多美女躍躍欲試的時候，時尚女子不得不提醒大家，在想著成果時，要看看風險，知道整型的風險嗎？大大小小風險不一而足：

infection 感染

excessive or unexpected bleeding 大出血

blood clots 血塊

tissue death 組織壞死

delayed healing 癒合遲緩

anesthesia risks （including shock, respiratory failure, drug or allergic reactions, cardiac arrest, coma, death）麻醉風險（包括休克、呼吸系統障礙、藥物或過敏反應、心跳停止、昏迷、死亡）

pneumonia 肺炎

loss or change of sensation 感官缺失

need for secondary surgeries / dissatisfaction with results 需二次手術或手術結果不理想

paralysis or less severe nerve damage 癱瘓或者較輕微的神經受損

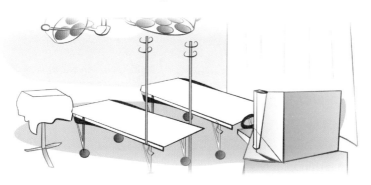

我想隆鼻。

I want to get a ***nose job**.

I want to have my nose done.

I'd like to get my nose reshaped.

學學老外這麼說

A：I want to get a nose job.

B：Your nose is pretty.

A：No, it's not. It's too flat, wide, and fat.

A：我想隆鼻。

B：你的鼻子挺好看的。

A：不好看。它又平，又寬，又大。

---

* nose job 隆鼻；學名 rhinoplasty。

MP3
202

她的塌鼻子變成了挺直的希臘鼻。

這句可以這麼說

Her *snub nose* is now a straight Grecian nose.

She turned her ***pug nose** into a straight Greek nose.

The bridge of her nose is a lot higher now.

學學老外這麼說

A : She turned her pug nose into a straight Greek nose.

B : Yeah, she used to have a snub nose.

A : 她的塌鼻子變成了挺直的希臘鼻。

B : 對,她以前是塌鼻子。

---

* snub nose 短翹鼻;塌鼻子。

* pug nose 塌鼻子(pug 哈巴狗)。

鼻子的類型

The Roman or aquiline nose: It is like a hook, known as a "hooknose".
（羅馬鼻 / 鷹鉤鼻：形狀似鉤，因此得名。）

The Grecian or straight nose: It is straight, with no curves or hooked shape. （希臘鼻 / 直鼻：直而沒有弧度和鉤狀。）

The Nubian nose: It is narrow at the top, and broad at the middle and the end, with wide nostrils. （努比亞鼻：上窄，中下寬，鼻孔大；通常黑人較常有此特徵。）

The snub nose: It is short in length, not sharp, hooked, or wide. （短翹鼻 / 塌鼻子：鼻子長度短，不尖、不鉤也不寬。）

The turned up nose / celestial nose: It runs continuously from the eyes towards the tip. （朝天鼻：鼻子和眼睛幾乎平行。）

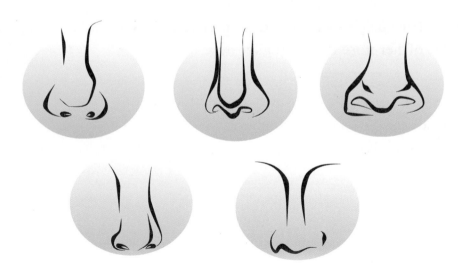

繡唇線能保持多長時間？

這句可以這麼說

How long does lip embroidery last?

How long will embroidered lip color stay?

學學老外這麼說

A：How long does embroidered lip color stay?

B：Up to 2 years.

A：繡唇能保持多長時間？

B：兩年以上。

我想試試漂唇。

I want to try *lip bleaching.
I want to bleach my lips.
I want to have my lips bleached.

A : My lips are too dark. I want to have them bleached.
B : You need to be careful about the side effects.

A : 我的嘴唇顏色太深，我想去漂唇。
B : 你要小心它的副作用。

---

* lip bleaching 漂唇。

做豐唇手術的人越來越多了。

這句可以這麼說

More and more people are having ***lip augmentation** surgery.

Lip augmentation surgeries are becoming more and more popular.

學學老外這麼說

A : My lips are too thin. I'm gonna have lip augmentation to get a pouty mouth.

B : I've heard about breast augmentation, but never lip augmentation.

A : Lip augmentation surgeries are becoming more and more popular.

A : 我的嘴唇太薄了。我要做豐唇手術,變成性感翹唇。

B : 我聽說過豐胸,但還沒聽說過豐唇手術。

A : 做豐唇手術的人越來越多了。

---

* lip augmentation 豐唇手術。

據說瑞絲朗玻尿酸能去皺紋，還能豐唇。

這句可以這麼說

I've heard that Restylane injections not only smooth wrinkles, but also **sculpt** lips.

I heard Restylane injections can reduce wrinkles and create fuller lips.

Restylane injections are recommended for wrinkles and lip sculpturing.

學學老外這麼說

A : I heard Restylane injections can reduce wrinkles and create fuller lips.

B : It depends on your skin type and other conditions.

A : 據說瑞絲朗玻尿酸能去皺紋和豐唇。

B : 得看你的膚質和其他條件而定。

單字

sculpt [skʌlpt] v.
雕塑；使立體

MP3-207

打肉毒桿菌有風險嗎？

這句可以這麼說

Are there any risks with Botox injections?

What are the dangers of Botox injections?

What are the *side effects of Botox injections?

學學老外這麼說

A : I heard Botox injections can thin the face. Are there any risks?

B : Yes. You may suffer from headaches, nausea, facial pain, **twitching** of the eyes, or even muscle weakness. The wrong **dosage** may even lead to death.

A : 我聽說打肉毒桿菌能瘦臉，有風險嗎？

B : 有。你可能會頭疼、噁心、臉疼、眼部痙攣，甚至肌肉無力。劑量不對會致死。

---

* side effect 副作用。

單字

twitch [twɪtʃ] v. 抽動；抽搐

dosage [ˋdosɪdʒ] n. 劑量

30-40 years

Heidi has a heart attack and is taken to the hospital. While on the operating table, she has a near death experience, during which she sees God and asks if this is the end for her.

God says no and explains that she has another 30-40 years to live.

As soon as she recovers, Heidi figures that since she's got another 30 or 40 years, she might as well stay in the hospital and have the face-lift, liposuction, breast augmentation, and tummy tuck that she has always promised herself. So she does, and she even changes the colour of her hair!

But tragedy strikes some weeks later. As Heidi is leaving hospital, she is knocked over and killed by a car.

When Heidi arrives in front of God, she asks, "I thought you said I had another 30-40 years?"

God replies, "I didn't recognize you."

30 到 40 年的壽命

海蒂心臟病突發住院,差點死在手術台上。手術過程中她看到了上帝,於是就問她是不是陽壽已盡。

上帝說不是,說她還有三十到四十年的壽命。

一恢復健康,海蒂想想自己還能活三十到四十年,不如繼續住院,把自己一直夢想的拉皮、抽脂、豐胸和腹部拉皮手術都一起做了。甚至連頭髮也染成了另一種顏色。

但是悲劇發生了——幾個星期以後,正當海蒂出院時,她被一輛車撞死了。

當海蒂來到上帝面前時,她問道:「我以為你說我還能活三十到四十年?」

上帝回答說:「我沒有認出你來。」

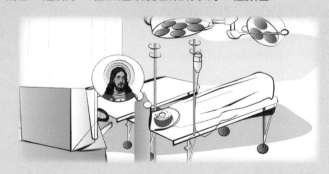

4 健康

Chapter

看看現代都市人的生活：「大吃大喝（binge eating and drinking）」太平常，大把鈔票在「健身房（gym）」，「極限運動（extreme sports）」當家常飯，「心理治療（therapy）」偷偷看。請看看時尚女子的健康打油詩：

美食長肚腩，（Yummy foods become tummy fat.）

菸酒催人老。（Smoking and drinking make you old.）

減肥不容易，（It is hard to lose weight.）

運動不能少。（And you need to work out.）

若要健康在，（If you want to look fit,）

還要心情好！（You have to keep in a good mood!）

MP3
208

我是個美食主義者。

這句可以這麼說

I am a **gourmand**.

I am a **foodie**.

學學老外這麼說

A：I am a foodie. I have a foodie blog.

B：Really? I'd like to read it.

A：我是個美食主義者。我有一個美食部落格。

B：真的嗎？我想拜讀一下。

單字

gourmand
[ˋgurmand] n.
講究飲食的；美食主義者

foodie [fudɪ] n.
（口）美食主義者

MP3
209

太好吃了！

這句可以這麼說

How delicious!

How tasty!

How **yummy**!

This is really mouth-watering.

What a **scrumptious** meal!

學學老外這麼說

A : How yummy! These are all my favorite home-style foods.

B : They're usually healthy, too.

A : 太好吃了！這些都是我最喜歡的家常菜。

B : 它們也都很健康。

單字

yummy [ˈjʌmɪ] adj.
好吃的，美味的

ptious[ˈskrʌmpʃəs]
adj.（口）非常美味
的；極好的

MP3
210

今天叫的外賣難以下嚥。

這句可以這麼說

Today's ***take-away** is **inedible**.

Today's take-away tastes terrible.

Today's take-away ***tastes like cardboard**.

Today's take-away is really **bland**.

學學老外這麼說

A : Today's take-away is really bland.

B : Pack your own lunch next time. We have a microwave.

A : 今天的外賣難吃死了。

B : 下次自己帶便當吧！我們有微波爐。

---

* take-away 外賣；盒飯。

* taste like cardboard 味同嚼蠟。

單字

inedible [ɪn`ɛdəbl] adj. 難以下嚥的

bland [blænd] adj. 沒滋味的；沒味道的

The Diet and Skipping

A blonde is terribly overweight, so her doctor puts her on a diet. "I want you to eat regularly for two days, then skip a day, and repeat this procedure for two weeks. The next time I see you, you'll have lost at least five pounds."
When the blonde returns, she's lost nearly 20 pounds. "Why, that's amazing!" the doctor says. "Did you follow my instructions?"
The blonde nods. "I'll tell you, though, I thought I was going to drop dead that third day."
"From hunger, you mean?" asked the doctor.
"No, from skipping."

節食和跳繩

有個金髮美女太胖了，所以她的醫生讓她節食。「我希望你能正常飲食兩天，然後跳過一天，重複這個過程兩個星期。下次我再見到你時，你肯定能瘦五磅。」
金髮美女再來時，瘦了近二十磅。「哇，太棒了！」醫生說：「你有照我的要求做嗎？」
金髮美女點頭道：「但我告訴你，每到第三天的時候我都覺得我會猝死。」
「你是說因為飢餓？」醫生問。
「不是，是因為跳繩。」
註：此處醫生意指第三天不吃飯，skip（跳過）一天，金髮美女卻誤解成跳繩（skip）跳一天。

273

我沒什麼胃口。

這句可以這麼說

I've lost my **appetite**.

I just don't feel like eating.

I have no stomach for food.

學學老外這麼說

A：I have lost my appetite.

B：But you haven't been eating anything since this morning.

A：我沒胃口。

B：可是你從早上到現在都沒吃東西。

單字

appetite

[ˋæpə͵taɪt] n. 胃口

我喜歡吃希臘菜。

這句可以這麼說

I love Greek **cuisine**.

I prefer Greek cuisine.

My favorite is Greek cuisine.

學學老外這麼說

A：I love Greek cuisine, especially *Kebab.

B：Kebab is actually Turkish.

A：我喜歡希臘菜，尤其是沙威瑪。

B：沙威瑪其實源自土耳其。

單字

cuisine [kwɪˋzin] n.
風味；烹調法

---

* Kebab [kəˋbɑb] n. 沙威瑪；土耳其烤肉

時尚情報站

高熱量的西方節日大餐

佳節美食太誘人，看看西方過節有哪些美味，熱量都不少哦！

turkey 火雞

stuffing inside the turkey 填料火雞

eggnog 蛋奶酒

peanut brittle 花生糖

gravy made with fat drippings 濃稠肉湯

candied sweet potatoes 蜜餞番薯

mashed potatoes 馬鈴薯泥

potato latkes 馬鈴薯餅

prime rib 上等肋排

pecan pie 核桃餡餅

MP3 213

哪些是高熱量食物？

這句可以這麼說

What are some high-**calorie** foods?

What foods are high in calories?

學學老外這麼說

A : What foods are high in calories?

B : Hamburgers, **tacos**, *trail mix, and eggnog, to name a few.

A : 哪些是高熱量食物？

B : 漢堡、墨西哥捲餅、什錦堅果，還有蛋奶酒等等。

單字

calorie [ˋkælərɪ] n. 卡路里（熱量單位）

taco [ˋtɑko] n. 墨西哥捲餅

---

* trail mix 什錦堅果。

快樂生活諺語

He is wise that knows when he is well enough. He is happy that thinks himself so. （知足為智者。自樂者常樂。）

Cheerfulness is health; its opposite, melancholy, is a disease. （歡樂就是健康，憂鬱即為病痛。）

It is not work that kills, but worry. （工作不傷身，傷身乃憂慮。）

Blessed is the person who is too busy to worry in the daytime, and too sleepy to worry at night. （白天忙得沒有時間發愁，夜裡睏得來不及發愁的人，才是真正幸福的人。）

Laugh, and the world laughs with you; weep, and you weep alone. （歡笑，則世界與你同樂；哭泣，則獨自悲傷。）

He who lives with his memories becomes old. He who lives with plans for the future remains young. （終日懷舊催人老，計畫未來保青春。）

要多吃含纖維的食物。

Eat more **fiber**.

Include more fiber in your diet.

Eat more high fiber foods.

學學老外這麼說

A : I don't like vegetables.

B : Honey, you need more high fiber foods. It's good for you.

A：我不喜歡蔬菜。

B：親愛的，你要多吃點高纖維食物。對身體好。

單字

fiber ['faɪbɚ] n. 纖維

MP3
215

你有點營養過剩。

Your problem is **overnutrition**.
Your nutrition ***intake** is too high.

A : Is it **malnutrition**?
B : You are actually overnutritioned. You need to
　　follow a special ***diet** from now on.

A：是不是營養不良？
B：事實上，你是營養過剩。從現在開始你需要特別的飲食法。

單字

overnutrition
[ˋovɚnuˋtrɪʃən] n.
營養過剩

malnutrition
[͵mælnuˋtrɪʃən] n. 營養不良

---

* intake [ˋɪn͵tek] v.（食物、飲料等的）攝取量
* diet 當動詞是「節食；依規定飲食」。當名詞時則指「日常食物」。

MP3
216

你的飲食不健康。

這句可以這麼說

You have a very unhealthy diet.

Your diet is high in calories and low in nutrition.

You need to change to a healthier diet.

You need to eat a more balanced diet.

學學老外這麼說

A : How can I lose some extra pounds?

B : In the first place, you really need to pay attention to your diet. Your diet is high in calories and low in nutrition.

A : 我要怎麼做才能多減幾磅的體重？

B : 首先，你要注意你的飲食。你吃的食物熱量太高，營養成分卻不夠。

 時尚情報站

騙人的食品標籤

少買加工食品，瞧瞧那些看似健康的食品標籤背後隱藏了什麼？

fat free 不含脂肪	→	Fat free, but full of sugar and chemicals. 不含脂肪，但含大量糖和化學物質。
reduced fat 少脂肪	→	Reduced fat, but increased carbohydrates. 減少了脂肪，但增加了碳水化合物。
low fat 低脂肪	→	Low fat, but high glycemic index. 低脂肪，但高血糖指數。
sugar free 無糖	→	Sugar free, but artificial everything else. 無糖，但有各種人工添加劑。
no added sugar 不添加糖	→	No added sugar... because the all-natural version has enough sugar to give you type II diabetes anyway. 不添加糖，因為所含天然糖分已足夠讓你得糖尿病。
diet 減肥的	→	"Diet" food, but it causes cancer in lab rats, so don't drink / eat too much of it. 減肥食品，但它會使白老鼠致癌，別吃或喝太多。

Misleading product lables
Fat Free
Reduced Fat
Low Fat
Sugar Free
No Added Sugar
Diet

MP3
217

我經常不吃早餐。

這句可以這麼說

I often skip breakfast.

I usually don't eat breakfast.

I don't eat breakfast very often.

學學老外這麼說

A : I often get up late and have to skip breakfast.

B : That's bad for your *digestive system and your health.

A : 我經常晚起所以不吃早餐。

B : 這對你的消化系統和健康不好。

---

* digestive [daɪˈdʒɛstɪv] adj. 消化的；和消化有關的。

吃飯要細嚼慢嚥。

Eat slowly.

Slow down when eating.

Don't ***gulp down** your food.

Don't ***wolf down** your food.

A : Stop wolfing down your food.

B : Why?

A : Don't you want to lose weight? You eat less when
you eat slowly.

A：吃慢一點，別狼吞虎嚥。

B：為什麼呢？

A：你不是想減肥嗎？吃得慢就會吃得少。

---

* glup down 咕嚕咕嚕大口吃喝。

* wolf down 狼吞虎嚥。

一忙起來我就不能正常吃飯。

I can't have *regular meals when I'm busy.

I have to grab a quick bite to eat when I'm busy.

I am too busy to have regular meals

A : I am too busy to have regular meals these days.

B : Just prepare some *ready meals like shepherds pie, lasagne, or pizza.

A : 我最近忙到都沒吃正餐。

B : 那就準備一些即食餐像是馬鈴薯鮮肉派，義大利千層麵或者是披薩。

---

* regular meal 指種類齊全、營養均衡的一餐。

* ready meal 類似台灣超商販售的便當類熟食，顧客買回家後只要加熱即可食用。

怎樣才能控制暴飲暴食的衝動？

Clinic

這句可以這麼說

How can I stop the urge to go on *an eating binge*?

How can I curb food *cravings*?

How can I control an emotional eating disorder?

學學老外這麼說

A : I binge on things like cookies and chips rather than fruit. How can I curb such cravings?

B : Snack regularly and don't skip meals. You'll feel hungry less often.

A : 我會沒有節制地狂吃餅乾和薯條這類不似水果的（不健康）東西。怎樣才能控制這種亂吃的衝動？

B : 吃零食要能節制，一定要吃正餐，這樣就不會那麼容易餓。

---

* binge [bɪndʒ] n. & v. 大吃大喝。 an eating binge 暴飲暴食。

* craving [ˋkrevɪŋ] n. 強烈的欲望。

她經常喝得大醉。

這句可以這麼說

She often goes on *a drinking binge.

She is a big binge drinker.

She is a heavy drinker.

She often gets drunk.

She often abuses alcohol.

學學老外這麼說

A : Good heavens! She *drinks like a fish.

B : She is a party girl and a big binge drinker.

A : How can she ruin her own health like that?

A : 天哪！她太能喝了。

B : 她是個派對女郎，還是個酒鬼。

A : 她怎麼能這樣糟蹋自己的健康呢？

---

* a drinking binge 酗酒；大量喝酒。

* drink like a fish 喝很多酒；很會喝酒。

她得了厭食症。

這句可以這麼說

She's got an eating disorder.

She has **anorexia**.

She ***suffers from** anorexia.

She is ***anorexic**.

學學老外這麼說

A : Your friend is really skinny.

B : Yeah, she is suffering from anorexia. It's all because of her weight-loss craze.

A : 你朋友瘦得像皮包骨。

B : 是啊，她得了厭食症，都是因為她想減肥想瘋了。

> **單字**
> **anorexia**
> [ˌænəˋrɛksɪə] n.
> （醫）厭食症

* suffer from 因疾病等而不舒服；因⋯⋯而受苦。
* anorexic [ˌænəˋrɛksɪk] n. 厭食者。

飲食壞習慣的後果

You're a serious snacker. → Overeating　（你太愛吃零食。→ 吃得過多。）

You're a speed-eater.→ Stomach troubles like bloating and indigestion. （你吃得太快。→ 胃出問題，例如胃脹氣和消化不良。）

You eat your way out of a bad mood. → A cycle of more bad moods and steady weight gain. （心情不好就吃東西。→ 進入心情更糟糕的惡性循環，且體重漸增。）

You eat carefully all week, then blow it on the weekend. → You undo five days of good. （你週一至週五都吃得很規律，到週末就暴飲暴食。→ 前五天的努力都浪費了。）

All your meals come in cans, bags, or boxes. → Unhealthy fats, sugar, salt, and excess calories. （你所有的食物都是罐裝、袋裝和盒裝的。→ 不健康的脂肪、糖、鹽和過量卡路里。）

You eat on the run. → Feel dissatisfied and have an upset stomach. （邊走邊吃。→ 感覺沒吃飽和胃不舒服。）

You're a mindless muncher. → Overeating when surfing the web and watching the tube. （你不知不覺吃了太多零食。→ 上網和看電視時吃得過多。）

You skip breakfast. → A lousy morning and overeating later on. （不吃早餐。→ 上午過得無精打采且之後吃得更多。）

You're a sugar fiend.→ A sugar crash. （你嗜糖如命。→ 吃糖後沒精神。）

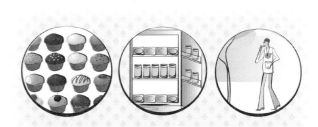

抽菸會使皮膚衰老。

Smoking leads to wrinkles.

Smoking leads to skin aging.

Smoking ages skin more than anything else.

Smoking speeds up the aging of your skin.

A：You smoke 2 packs of cigarettes a day? Smoking causes wrinkles to your skin.

B：I know, but I just don't know how to quit.

A：你每天抽兩包菸？抽菸會讓你的皮膚長皺紋。

B：我知道，但我就是戒不掉。

膠原蛋白美容飲料很有效。

Collagen drinks work well.

Collagen beauty drinks are really effective.

Collagen drinks do have anti-aging effects.

A : Do collagen drinks have real anti-aging effects?

B : As I know, they're very ***popular with** Japanese women.

A : 膠原蛋白美容飲料真有抗老的功能嗎？

B : 據我了解，它很受日本女性喜愛。

單字

collagen
[ˋkɑlədʒən] n.
膠原蛋白

---

* popular with 受……歡迎。

抗氧化食物可以抗老。

onions, radishes, papaya, olives

MP3 225

這句可以這麼說

Antioxidant foods are good age defying foods.

Antioxidant means anti-aging.

Antioxidant foods help to keep your skin young.

學學老外這麼說

A : I hear that antioxidant foods help to keep your skin young. What foods are high in antioxidants?

B : Many vegetables and fruits contain antioxidants, such as onions, radishes, papayas, and olives.

A : 聽說抗氧化食物可以抗老。什麼食物富含抗氧化成分？

B : 很多蔬菜水果都含抗氧化物，例如：洋蔥、蘿蔔、木瓜和橄欖。

單字

antioxidant
[ˌæntɪˋɑksədənt] n.
抗氧化劑

黑木耳能排毒還能養顏美容。

這句可以這麼說

*Black fungus** can cleanse the body of **toxins** and nurture the skin.

Black fungus has **detoxifying** and beautifying effects.

Black fungus can cleanse your small intestine.

學學老外這麼說

A : Black fungus again! Can we have something else?

B : It's good for cleansing your small *intestines**.

A : 又吃黑木耳！能不能換點別的？

B : 它能清理你的小腸。

* black fungus 黑木耳。

* intestines [ɪn`tɛstɪns] n. 腸

單字

toxin [`taksɪn] n.
毒素

detoxify
[di`taksə‚faɪ] v.
排毒；解毒

喝玫瑰花茶能美白。

―――【 這句可以這麼說 】――――

Rose herbal tea has good whitening effects.

Rose herbal tea whitens the skin.

It says rose herbal tea is as good as a whitening mask.

―――【 學學老外這麼說 】―――――

A : It says rose herbal tea is as good as a whitening
　　mask.

B : Really? I'll have to try it.

A : 聽說喝玫瑰花茶和美白面膜的效果一樣好。

B : 真的嗎？我要試試。

有必要吃補品嗎？

這句可以這麼說

Are these really *must-have supplements?

Are supplements necessary for health?

Do we really need to take supplements?

學學老外這麼說

A : Do I really need all these vitamin supplements?

B : Of course. You are not getting enough fruits and vegetables.

A : 我真的需要吃這麼多維他命營養品嗎？

B : 當然，你蔬菜水果吃得太少了。

單字

supplement
[`sʌpləmənt] n. 補品

---

* must-have 基本必備的。

MP3
229

動物內臟富含卵磷脂。

Large amounts of DHA are found in animal organs.
Animal organs are rich in DHA.
Animal organs are high in DHA.

A : Animal organs are high in cholesterol.
B : But, they are also rich in DHA. And DHA has anti-
aging effects.

A : 動物內臟含高膽固醇。

B : 但也富含卵磷脂，卵磷脂有抗老功效。

美女食譜

有句俗話說，「吃什麼像什麼。（You are what you eat.）」美女也是吃出來的。時尚女子教你抗老三要素！

1. 含「矽」的食物能延緩肌膚和頭髮的衰老：

bell pepper （彩椒）　　　　　burdock root （牛蒡）

cucumber （黃瓜）　　　　　　horsetail （馬尾草）

marjoram （牛至）　　　　　　radish （蘿蔔）

New Zealand Spinach （紐西蘭波菜）　romaine lettuce （蘿蔓生菜）

tomato （番茄）

2.「抗氧化」食物永保青春：

cruciferous vegetables（十字花科蔬菜）

arugula（芝麻菜）

nettle leaves（蕁麻葉）

watercress（西洋菜）

radish（蘿蔔）

papaya（木瓜）

ripe peppers（紅辣椒）

burdock root （牛蒡）

acerola berry（針葉櫻桃）

onion（洋蔥）

olive（橄欖和橄欖油）

wheat germ oil（小麥胚芽油）

3.「清腸」食物排毒養顏：

green superfood（螺旋藻）

beets（根莖類食物）

shiitake mushrooms（椎茸／香菇）

apple（蘋果）

papaya（木瓜）

kefir（發酵乳）

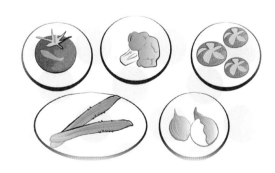

MP3
230

你經常運動嗎？

這句可以這麼說

Do you often *work out?

How often do you exercise?

How often do you work out?

Do you exercise regularly?

學學老外這麼說

A : Do you often work out?

B : Not really. Maybe I should.

A : 你經常運動嗎？

B : 沒有。或許我該多做些運動。

---

* work out 做大量的運動。

MP3 231

你的身材真棒。

這句可以這麼說

You look fit.

You have a shapely figure.

You're *in good **shape**.

You've got the right **curves**.

學學老外這麼說

A : You used to have a shapely figure.

B : I am going to exercise more to *shape my body.

A : 你以前身材多好啊！

B : 我打算要多運動塑身。

單字

shapely [`ʃeplɪ] adj
（女子）身材勻稱的

curve [kɝv] n. 曲線

---

* in shape 健康；健美。

* shape one's body 塑身。

減肥要節食和運動相結合。

這句可以這麼說

You have to combine exercise with diet to lose weight.

You'll lose weight if you exercise and *go on a diet.

學學老外這麼說

A : I have been on a diet for a month, but nothing has happened.

B : You need to combine exercise with a diet.

A：我已經節食快一個月了，可是什麼效果也沒有。

B：你需要把運動和節食結合在一起。

---

* go on a diet 節食。

MP3
233

跳舞對減肥很有幫助。

這句可以這麼說

Dancing is a good way to lose weight.

Dancing is a very good *weight loss exercise.

Dancing can really help you *slim down.

學學老外這麼說

A : I just joined a dancing weight loss program.

B : I can't wait to see the changes. Dancing can really
help you slim down.

A：我加入了一個跳舞減肥課。

B：我等不及想看看你的變化，跳舞對減肥很有幫助。

---

* weight loss 減肥。

* slim [slɪm] adj. 苗條的。slim down（靠節食等）變苗條。

MP3
234

我要訂一個健身減肥計畫。

I am going to draw up a weight loss exercise plan.
I'm going to set up a workout plan to lose weight.
What I need is a weight loss exercise plan.

A : I am going to draw up a weight loss exercise plan to lose 5 pounds.

B : You can join a weight loss program at the Beauty gym.

A : 我想訂一個健身減肥五磅的計畫。

B : 你可以直接參加美女健身房的減肥活動。

五個可以幫助燃燒脂肪的習慣

Walk 10,000 steps every day. （每天走一萬步。）

Do a housework workout. （勤做家事鍛鍊身體。）

Eat breakfast to speed up your metabolism. （吃早餐促進代謝。）

Drink eight glasses of water every day. （每天要喝八杯水。）

Turn down the heat to burn more calories. （暖氣關小可以多燃燒脂肪。）

小笑話一則

In-laws

A couple drove several miles down a country road in total silence. Neither said a word to the other. An earlier discussion had led to an argument, and neither wanted to concede. As they passed a barnyard full of mules and pigs, the wife sarcastically asked, "Relatives of yours?" "Yep," the husband replied, "in-laws".

姻親

一對夫妻在鄉間小路上開車走了好幾哩都沉默不語。之前他們在討論問題時吵了起來，誰也不想認輸，雙方一句話都沒有說。當他們經過一片圈著騾子和豬的空地時，妻子諷刺道：「這是你的親戚吧？」「是啊，」丈夫回答，「是姻親。」

你喜歡室外還是室內運動？

這句可以這麼說

Which do you prefer, outdoor or indoor sports?

Do you like outdoor or indoor workouts?

Do you prefer to exercise outdoors, or indoors?

學學老外這麼說

A：Do you prefer to exercise outdoors, or indoors?

B：Outdoors. I can breathe some fresh air and get some sun.

A：你喜歡室外還是室內運動？

B：室外運動，我可以呼吸多一點新鮮空氣和晒晒太陽。

MP3
236

我每週去一次健身房。

I go to the gym once a week.
I work out in the gym once a week.

A : How often do you work out?
B : I go to the gym once a week.

A : 你多久運動一次？
B : 我每週去一次健身房。

MP3 237

那家健身房的設備器材不錯。

這句可以這麼說

That gym is well-equipped.

They have decent equipment at that gym.

The equipment is good at that gym.

學學老外這麼說

A : What do you think about that gym?

B : The equipment is good. So is the membership fee.

A：那家健身房如何？

B：設備不錯，入會價格也合理。

MP3
238

我辦了張健身會員卡。

這句可以這麼說

I bought a gym membership.

I got a gym membership.

I got a membership card for this gym.

學學老外這麼說

A：I just bought a gym membership.

B：How much is it?

A：100 dollars for half a year.

A：我辦了張健身會員卡。

B：多少錢？

A：半年一百元美金。

MP3
239

我想退掉我的健身卡。

I want to cancel my gym membership.
I want to quit the gym.

A : My gym membership is making only my wallet
   skinnier. I want to cancel it.

B : You seldom work out there. Just do it.

A : 我辦的健身卡只讓我的錢包變扁而已，我想把它退掉。

B : 反正你很少去健身房，就退掉吧！

Home Gym 家有健身房

不想去擁擠的健身房，在家就能健身，需要買什麼器材呢？

男士們可能需要「引體向上支架」（chin bar）、「槓鈴」（barbell），「仰臥起坐板」（sit-ups board）和「史密斯訓練架」（Smith Machine）等。那麼時尚女子們需要什麼健身器材呢？

starter kit 初學者系列

dumbbells 啞鈴

jump rope 跳繩

stability ball 健身球

resistance tubing 彈性拉力繩

mat 墊子

professional kit 專業系列

adjustable bench 可調式啞鈴椅

tread mill 跑步機

recumbent stationary bike 臥式固定自行車

MP3
240

你平常做什麼運動？

這句可以這麼說

What exercises do you usually do?

How do you work out?

What kinds of sports do you usually play?

學學老外這麼說

A : What exercises do you usually do?

B : I do *sit-ups, *pushups, and *weights.

A : 你平常都做什麼運動？

B : 仰臥起坐、伏地挺身，還有重量訓練。

---

* sit-ups 仰臥起坐。

* pushup = press up 伏地挺身。

* do weights（口）重量訓練。

我很多同事每天競走當作運動。

這句可以這麼說

Many of my colleagues go ***power walking** every day.

Many of my colleagues go for brisk walks every day.

Several of my colleagues do ***walking sprints** every day.

學學老外這麼說

A : Is there a simple way to lose weight?

B : Many of my colleagues go power walking every day.

A : 有沒有什麼簡單的減肥方式？

B : 我很多同事每天競走當作運動。

---

* power walking 競走。

* walking sprints 快走。

MP3
242

我每天都做仰臥起坐。

I do sit-ups every day.

Sit-ups are part of my daily routine.

A : I can do 100 sit-ups* **in a row**.

B : No wonder you have a ***six-pack**.

A：我能一口氣做一百個仰臥起坐。

B：難怪你有六塊腹肌呢。

---

* in a row 連續不斷地。

* six pack 六塊腹肌。

MP3
243

瑜伽難嗎？

Is yoga difficult?

Is yoga difficult to perform?

Are yoga postures difficult?

A : I just bought a yoga mat. Is yoga difficult?

B : You can start from easier postures and then go on
to more difficult ones.

A : 我剛買了一個瑜伽墊。瑜伽難嗎？

B : 你可以從容易的姿勢開始，然後慢慢到有難度的。

歐洲很流行體適能瑜伽。

這句可以這麼說

Power yoga is the most popular type in Europe.

Power yoga is in vogue now in Europe.

Europeans prefer power yoga.

學學老外這麼說

A : What type of yoga are you practicing?

B : Power yoga. It is in vogue now in Europe.

A ：你在練哪種瑜伽？

B ：體適能瑜伽。它現在在歐洲很流行。

你想參加有氧健身班嗎？

這句可以這麼說

Do you want to enroll in an *__aerobics__ class?

Do you want to attend the aerobics class?

Are you interested in the aerobics class?

學學老外這麼說

A : Why don't you attend an aerobics class?

B : Does it help burn calories?

A : Of course, if you keep doing it.

A : 你為什麼不去參加有氧健身班呢？

B : 能燃燒脂肪減肥嗎？

A : 當然，如果你能持續。

---

* aerobics [ɛ`robɪks] n. 有氧運動；有氧舞蹈。

跳肚皮舞能瘦小腹嗎？

這句可以這麼說

Does ***belly dancing** give you a flat stomach?

Can belly dancing burn the belly fat?

Can I lose some belly fat through belly dancing?

Will I get a flat tummy by doing belly dancing?

學學老外這麼說

A : I just enrolled in a belly dancing course.

B : Does belly dancing give you a flat stomach?

A : I hope it will help me to regain my slim waistline and flat stomach.

A : 我剛剛報名參加肚皮舞班。

B : 跳肚皮舞能瘦小腹嗎？

A : 我希望肚皮舞能讓我重獲小蠻腰和平坦小腹。

---

* belly dance 肚皮舞。

MP3 247

現在粉領族流行跳鋼管舞。

這句可以這麼說

*__Pole dancing__ has become a new hobby for white-collar working women.

Pole dancing is really popular with white-collar working women.

Pole dancing is a new fitness choice for white-collar working women.

There is a new fitness ***craze for** pole dancing among white-collar working women.

學學老外這麼說

A : My girlfriend is talking about taking a pole dancing class! What can I do?

B : You are out now. Pole dancing is really popular with white-collar working women.

A : 我女朋友說她要去學跳鋼管舞！我該怎麼辦？

B : 你落伍了。現在粉領族很流行跳鋼管舞。

---

* pole dance 鋼管舞。

* craze for something 為某事而狂熱。

上班不忘健身

Make the most of your commute.（通勤路上不偷懶。）

Look for opportunities to stand.（多找機會站一站。）

Take fitness breaks.（活動身體稍休息。）

Trade your office chair for a fitness ball.（健身球代替辦公椅。）

Keep fitness equipment in your work area.（健身器材放辦公區。）

Get social and organize a walking group.（成立或加入走路團體。）

Conduct meetings on the go.（開會也能動起來。）

Pick up the pace when you walk.（走路時加快腳步。）

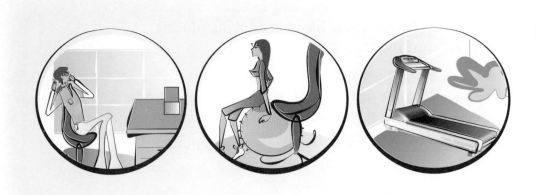

MP3
248

她很會溜冰。

這句可以這麼說

She is really good at *roller skating.
She is a good roller skater.

學學老外這麼說

A : Can you do roller skating or *in-line skating?
B : Both. But I prefer ice skating. I hope to try *figure
    skating some day.

A : 你會溜冰或者溜直排輪嗎？
B : 都會。但我喜歡真正的滑冰，我希望哪天能試試花式滑冰。

---

* roller skating 溜冰。
* in-line skating 溜直排輪。
* ice skating 滑冰。
* figure skating 花式滑冰。

我滑雪時扭到腳了。

這句可以這麼說

I *sprained my ankle** skiing.

I *twisted my ankle** while skiing.

學學老外這麼說

A : Why are you *limping**?

B : I twisted my ankle while skiing.

A : It's swollen.

A : 你怎麼一拐一拐的？

B : 我滑雪的時候扭傷了腳踝。

A : 都腫起來了。

---

* sprain / twist one's ankle 扭傷腳踝。

* limp [lɪmp] v. 跛行。

MP3
250

運動前做好熱身準備。

***Warm up** before exercising.

Warming up is very important before any exercise.

Stretching is necessary before exercising.

A : I threw out my back when I was working out
     yesterday.

B : Next time, do some warm-ups beforehand.

A：我昨天運動時把背部拉傷了。

B：下次運動前要先做熱身運動。

---

* warm up 熱身。

攀岩有什麼危險？

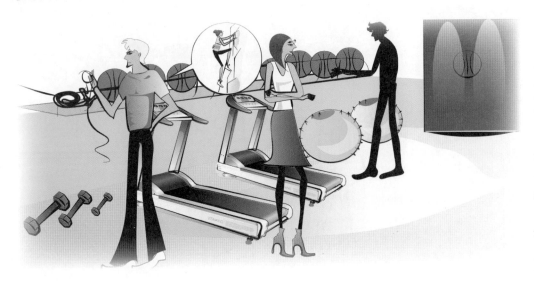

這句可以這麼說

Is *rock climbing dangerous?

How dangerous is rock climbing?

What are the risks of rock climbing?

學學老外這麼說

A : I'm going rock climbing this weekend. What are the
risks of rock climbing?

B : Don't you know there's a high risk of injury, and
even death?

A : Take it easy! It's indoor rock climbing.

A : 這週末我要去攀岩。攀岩有什麼危險？

B : 你不知道攀岩有很大的受傷率和死亡風險嗎？

A : 別緊張，只是室內攀岩。

---

* rock climbing 攀岩。

MP3
252

我不喜歡極限運動。

SUPERMARKET

I don't like ***extreme sports**.
I don't care for extreme sports.
I am no fan of extreme sports.

A : Would you like to join a ***skydiving** club?
B : That's a guy thing. I don't care for extreme sports.

A : 你想加入跳傘俱樂部嗎？
B : 那是男人玩的。我對極限運動沒興趣。

---

* extreme sports 極限運動。
* skydiving 高空跳傘。

323

MP3 253

你試過水肺潛水嗎？

Have you ever tried *scuba diving?

Do you have any scuba diving experience?

Is this your first time scuba diving?

學學老外這麼說

A : Do you have any scuba diving experience?

B : Isn't that a sport for tropical seas? Besides, I don't have an *air tank or **regulator**.

A : Well, you could just try it first in a swimming pool.

A : 你有試過水肺潛水嗎？

B : 那不是熱帶海邊玩的項目嗎？再說，我也沒有氧氣筒和呼吸設備。

A : 這個嘛，你可以先在游泳池裡試試。

單字

diving [ˈdaɪvɪŋ] n. 潛水

regulator [ˈrɛɡjəˌletə] n. 呼吸調節器

---

* scuba [ˈskjubə] n. 水肺。scuba diving 水肺潛水。

* air tank 氧氣筒。

高空彈跳真是太刺激了。

這句可以這麼說

***Bungee jumping** is really exciting.

Bungee jumping is ***exhilarating**.

Bungee jumping is thrilling.

學學老外這麼說

A : How did it feel when you went bungee jumping?

B : It was thrilling.

A : 高空彈跳時你有什麼感覺？

B : 太刺激了。

---

* bungee jumping 高空彈跳。

* exhilarating [ɪgˋzɪləˌretɪŋ] adj. 令人激動的。

十大極限運動

現在玩刺激的極限運動不再是男性專利，女性身影在極限運動中也處處可見。

skydiving 高空跳傘

surfing 衝浪

bungee jumping 高空彈跳

rock climbing 攀岩

mountain biking 極限越野單車

white-water kayaking 泛舟

windsurfing 風浪板運動

snowboarding 滑板滑雪

wakeboarding 滑水

scuba diving 水肺潛水

MP3 255

我最近壓力很大。

這句可以這麼說

I have been under a lot of pressure lately.

I'm feeling a lot of pressure these days.

I've been under a lot of stress recently.

I've been really *stressed out lately.

學學老外這麼說

A : I have two deadlines to meet next week. I am so stressed out.

B : Take it easy. Everything will fall into place.

A : 我下週要趕兩個結案時間。壓力大到快把我壓垮了。

B : 放輕鬆點，船到橋頭自然直。

---

* stressed out 壓力過大而累垮。

我快累死了。

這句可以這麼說

I am beat.

I am dead tired

I am exhausted.

I am worn out.

I feel so **drained**.

學學老外這麼說

A : Look at the dark circles under your eyes. You look so **bushed**.

B : I stayed up really late again. I feel so drained.

A : You need to go to a spa and get a massage.

A：看看你的熊貓眼。你看起來筋疲力盡了。

B：我又熬夜熬得很晚，快累死了。

A：你需要做個 spa，按摩一下。

單字

drain [dren] v.
精力耗盡

bushed [buʃt] adj.
（口）筋疲力盡的

328

我昨晚一夜沒睡。

這句可以這麼說

I couldn't get to sleep last night.

I *didn't sleep a wink** last night.

I had a sleepless night last night.

I *tossed and turned** all night.

學學老外這麼說

A : You look so pale.

B : I didn't sleep a wink last night.

A : You have too much on your mind.

A：你臉色看起來很蒼白。

B：我昨晚一夜沒睡。

A：你操心的事太多了。

---

* not sleep a wink 完全沒睡覺。

* toss and turn 輾轉難眠。

你需要看心理醫生嗎？

這句可以這麼說

Do you need **therapy**?

Do you need counseling?

Do you need to see a **therapist**?

學學老外這麼說

A：I am suffering from severe *insomnia.

B：Do you need to see a therapist?

A：I don't know if that will help.

A：我深受嚴重的失眠之苦。

B：你需要看心理醫生嗎？

A：不知道會不會有幫助。

單字

therapy [ˈθɛrəpɪ]
n. 心理治療

therapist
[ˈθɛrəpɪst] n.
心理醫生

---

* insomnia [ɪnˈsɑmnɪə] n. 失眠症。

MP3
259

你要設法排解壓力。

這句可以這麼說

You have to find a way to relieve your stress.

You have to reduce your stress.

You need to let off some steam.

You need to lighten your load.

學學老外這麼說

A : I feel tired.

B : You need to let off some steam. Go to the beach
and *have a blast.

A : 我好累。

B : 你需要設法排解壓力。去海邊玩個痛快。

---

* have a blast（俚）玩個痛快。

MP3
260

你需要休息。

這句可以這麼說

You need to rest.

You need a break.

You need to take a break.

You need to take some time off.

學學老外這麼說

A : Are you ok?

B : I'm just **pooped**. My boss is so **pushy** about this project.

A : Take it easy and take a break.

A : 你還好吧？

B : 我已經筋疲力盡了，老闆對這個計畫要求太嚴苛了。

A : 放輕鬆點，休息一下。

單字

pooped [pupt] n.（俚）疲倦的；筋疲力盡的

pushy [ˋpʊʃɪ] adj. 堅持己見的；執意強求的

減壓小處方

Throw on some music and clean the house.（邊聽音樂邊打掃家裡。）

Watch the fish in an aquarium.（看魚缸裡的魚。）

Talk to a friend.（和朋友聊天。）

Sing along with music.（隨著音樂唱歌。）

Take a bubble bath.（洗個泡泡浴。）

Walk your dog.（遛狗。）

Try breathing exercises.（試試氣功。）

Draw a picture.（畫畫。）

Dance to your favorite music.（在你最喜歡的樂聲中起舞。）

Try yoga and meditation.（試試瑜伽和冥想。）

Play music and cook something wonderful.（一邊聽音樂一邊下廚準備美食。）

Take a nap.（小睡一會。）

你是不是有什麼心事？

這句可以這麼說

Are you worried about something?

Do you* **have something weighing on your mind**?

Is there something on your mind?

Is something bothering you?

學學老外這麼說

A : Are you all right? There must be something weighing on your mind.

B : Yeah, I failed my final exam.

A : Don't blame yourself. I heard that none of your classmates passed.

A : 你還好吧？你一定有心事。

B : 是的，我期末考考糟了。

A : 別責備自己了，我聽說你們同學沒有一個及格的。

---

* have something weighing on one's mind 為某事擔憂。

MP3
262

不要老想著這件事。

這句可以這麼說

Don't *dwell on* it.

Get your mind off it.

Don't give it another thought.

You need to *get over* this.

學學老外這麼說

A : Don't dwell on your interview anymore.

B : I just can't help it.

A：不要老想著你的面試。

B：我就是無法控制。

---

* dwell on 老是想著某事。

* get one's mind off something 使某人不再思考或擔憂某事物。

* get over 把⋯⋯忘懷。

你怎麼悶悶不樂的？

這句可以這麼說

Why are you so **glum**?

Why the long face?

Why so serious?

Why are you **moping**?

Why are you in such a bad mood?

You seem really down. What's up?

── 學學老外這麼說 ──

A : Why so serious? Did you get up on the wrong side of the bed this morning?

B : I lost money in the stock market again. I *feel really **down**.

A : *It happens. Better luck next time.

A : 幹嘛悶悶不樂的，早上下床下錯邊了嗎？

B : 玩股票又賠了，很鬱悶。

A : 這種事難免發生，下次就會轉運了。

---

* feel down 心情低落。

* It happens.（某事）難以避免；總可能發生。

單字

glum [glʌm] v.
（口）鬱悶的；
悶悶不樂的

mope [mop] v.
鬱鬱寡歡；意志消沉

MP3
264

要往好處想。

Look at the bright side.
Look for the *silver lining.
Stay positive.
Think positively.

A : Jenny refused to go out with me. No one will ever
love me. I'll die alone.
B : Look for the silver lining. What you don't know is
that someone has a crush on you.

A : 珍妮拒絕和我約會，沒有人會愛我。我會一個人孤老死去的。
B : 別這麼悲觀，搞不好有人在暗戀你喔。

---

* silver lining 出自諺語 Every cloud has a silver lining.（烏雲背後總有一
線光芒。）

開心點。

這句可以這麼說

Cheer up.

Lighten up.

Come on.

Be happy.

學學老外這麼說

A：What's the matter?

B：I lost my wallet.

A：That's too bad. Let me buy you a drink to cheer you
　　up.

A：怎麼了？

B：我錢包掉了。

A：真糟糕。我請你喝一杯，讓你開心點。

MP3
266

她是個很樂觀的人。

這句可以這麼說

She is very ***optimistic**.

She is very positive.

She has a positive attitude.

She always looks at the bright side.

學學老外這麼說

A : Jane is always smiling. Her smile brightens up a whole room like a beam of sunlight.

B : Yeah, she is a person who has found inner peace and has a positive attitude toward life.

A : 珍總是面帶微笑。她的微笑就像陽光一樣，讓整個房間都亮起來。

B : 是啊，她是個內心平靜的人，生活態度也很健康。

---

* optimistic [ˌɑptə`mɪstɪk] adj. 樂觀的。

如何保持好心情？

這句可以這麼說

How can I stay in a good mood?

How can I keep a good mood?

How can I put myself in a good mood?

How can I get myself back into a good frame of mind?

學學老外這麼說

A：Have you any tips to keep me in a good mood?

B：Be satisfied and forget about perfectionism.

A：有沒有什麼可以讓我保持好心情的撇步？

B：要知足，忘記所謂的完美主義。

Mental Health Hotline

Hello, welcome to the mental health hotline.

If you have obsessive compulsive disorder, press 1 repeatedly.

If you are co-dependent, please ask someone to press 2 for you.

If you have multiple personality syndrome, press 3, 4, 5, and 6.

If you suffer from paranoid schizophrenia, we know who you are and what you want. Stay on the line so we can trace your call.

If you are delusional, press 7, and your call will be transfer to the mothership.

If you are hearing voices, listen carefully, and a small voice will tell you which number to press.

If you are manic depressive, it doesn't matter which button you press. No one will answer anyway.

If you are dyslexic, press 96969696969696.

If you have a nervous disorder, please fidget with the pound button until a representative comes on the line.

If you have amnesia, press 8 and state your name, address, phone number, date of birth, social security number, and your mother's and grandmother's maiden names.

If you have post traumatic stress disorder, slowly and carefully press 911.

If you have bi-polar disorder, please leave a message after the beep. Or before the beep. Please wait for the beep.

If you have short-term memory loss, please call again in a few minutes.

If you have low self esteem, please hang up. All our representatives are busy.

心理健康熱線

您好，歡迎撥打心理健康專線。

如果您有強迫症，請不斷重複按 1。

如果您有人格依賴症，請讓別人替您按 2。

如果您有多重人格症候群，請按數字 3、4、5 和 6。

如果您有妄想型精神分裂症，我們知道您是誰以及您需要什麼。請不要掛電話，以便我們追蹤您的電話。

如果您有妄想症，請按 7，您的電話將被轉接到母艦。

如果您有幻聽，請仔細聽，將有一個小聲音告訴您按哪個數字。

如果您有躁鬱症，您按哪個數字都沒有關係，總之無人接聽。

如果您有閱讀障礙，請按 96969696969696。

如果您有神經錯亂，請不停亂按井字鍵，直到有專人前來接聽。

如果您有失憶症，請按 8，並說出您的名字、地址、電話號碼、出生日期、社會保險號碼和您母親和祖母的娘家姓氏。

如果您有創傷後壓力症候群，請慢慢地、小心地按 911。

如果您有躁鬱症，請在聽到嘟一聲後留言。或在嘟一聲前。請等待嘟一聲。

如果你有暫時失憶症，請在幾分鐘後再試撥一次。

如果您有自我貶低傾向，請掛斷。所有專員都很忙。

國家圖書館出版品預行編目資料

出國血拼，臨時需要的那句英文／夏建蘭作 .— 新北市：
希望星球語言，民 102.12
　　面；公分
ISBN 978-986-6045-47-9（平裝附光碟片）
1. 英語　2. 會話
805.188　　　　　　　　　　　　　　102024729

出國血拼，臨時需要的那句英文

作　　者：夏建蘭

審　　訂：John P. Ring・Bill Martin

插圖繪製：艾米 & 鈴鐺（波普）

總 編 輯：吳淑芬

責任編輯：余素維

資深編輯：李碧涵

特約編輯：陳佳聖、陳治宏

校　　對：賴逸娟、陳怡秀

法律顧問：朱應翔、徐立信律師

出　　版：希望星球語言出版

代　　理：漢皇國際文化有限公司

地　　址：235 新北市中和區建康路 150 號 3 樓

電　　話：(02) 2226-3070

傳　　真：(02) 2226-0198

E-mail：service.hopefulplanet@gmail.com

總 經 銷：易可數位行銷股份有限公司

地　　址：231 新北市新店區寶橋路 235 巷 6 弄 3 號 5 樓

電　　話：(02) 8911-0825

傳　　真：(02) 8911-0801

本版發行：102 年 12 月

定　　價：380 元

ISBN：978-986-6045-47-9

Copyright©2013 by HAN SHIAN Culture Publishing Co., Ltd, Taiwan,
R.O.C.